LAS VEGAS (and every casino in the world) was full of men and women like that gray-haired woman sitting at the slot machine in front of me. They all played for their own varied reasons, just like I, Poker Boy, played live poker for mine.

But it was said that men and women like her created the ghost slots. Or at least so the theory goes. At some point in the past, I was sure that someone had spent weeks, or even years, playing the Saturn Slots, begging them, cussing at them, talking to them, pleading with them, day in and day out. Those slots had become a person's life, had given them both joy and misery.

When some person gave a slot machine everything they had, the theory was that the machine took on a life of its own.

But like any slot machine, it must be fed. Only ghost slots don't need money, they need more life.

As I watched the old woman with the big black purse, she pulled out another ten-dollar bill and the machine ate it like a hungry animal.

She didn't even seem to notice.

IN

DEAN WESLEY SMITH

WMGPUBLISHING

The Slots of Saturn

Published 2015 by WMG Publishing
www.wmgpublishing.com
First published in a different form in *Smith's Monthly #7,* April, 2014
Cover and Layout copyright © 2015 by WMG Publishing
Cover design by Allyson Longueira/WMG Publishing
Cover art copyright © Trilingstudio/Dreamstime, Chudtsankov/Dreamstime
ISBN-13: 978-1-56146-609-2
ISBN-10: 1-56146-609-3

IN

··◆ *1* ◆··

A SUPERHERO ARRIVES

I LOVE CASINOS. Always have.

I mean I truly love them, like some people enjoy sitting beside a calm mountain lake. Walking into a casino, it feels like I have stepped on an ocean beach on a warm evening with no wind, combined with the at-home feel of sitting by a fire, under a nice reading light, with a warm drink and a good book.

I admit, casinos are loud, with both machine and people noises, and are designed by experts to take a person's money. Yet every time I step through the door into a casino, either in Vegas, Atlantic City, or in timbuck-six North Dakota, I know I am home, that I am safe, that I am in control of my surroundings.

As Poker Boy, when I am in a casino, I also have my superpowers. I have to be honest that I love that feeling as well.

My superpowers, which are needed by definition to be a super-hero, are varied. I have still not explored them all. Sometimes even I am surprised at what I can do.

As I stepped through the side door of Binion's Horseshoe Casino and Hotel in downtown Las Vegas, I walked right into the center of at least forty poker tables. I knew I had once again found my own little slice of heaven. I could feel the power flowing through me. My muscles, tense and tight from the long cab ride, relaxed as if rubbed by a Swedish hot-rub expert.

And trust me, Heidi, my Swedish hot-rub expert from two Vegas trips back, could relax the man of steel down into a pool of metal. Those fingers of hers were secret weapons and, I know for a fact and from wonderful memory, that she turned Poker Boy into Go Fish Man in two minutes.

I stopped and just took a deep breath of the smoke-tainted air of the old casino, filling my lungs with the poisons that killed others, but gave me strength.

Stopping just inside a casino front door was a habit of mine. Every time I went into a new casino, or an old one like the Horseshoe, I would just stop inside the door and look around, giving myself a few seconds to enjoy the feel. As Poker Boy, I get a lot of good feelings, especially when I have helped someone, but there are never enough of those good feelings in life, so I take my joys where I can get them. And stopping inside a casino door and just looking around was one of my joys in life.

Today, everything around me looked like a standard day in casino world.

On my right were some of the live poker games, on my left the overflow part of the tournament area, now with all the tables empty. The main desk for the hotel was beyond all the tables, and I had to get there by sort of following the yellow brick road of the pattern on the carpet, through the tables, down between the railings along the poker tables, and then through the ropes in the open area in front of the hotel desk.

Those ropes that guard the front desks of most hotels always made me feel like a cow being herded to the guy with the hammer who would hit me, put me out of my misery, and turn my body into prime rib and flank steaks. Some hotels had almost done that to me in the past.

There wasn't even anyone waiting in line to check in. Maybe I could avoid the ropes altogether and just go for the hammer.

I put my head down and moved toward the front desk, following the pattern on the carpet, hoping I could get checked in and to my room before anyone knew I was here. Even superheroes needed time to unwind from the traveling and the cab ride from the airport.

Actually, I was looking forward to taking a nap.

I somehow made it all the way to the front desk without being recognized. Granted, I am really not that famous, in a strict sense of the word. But I am often recognized across a crowded casino by someone who wants my help, like a dog in need to pee spotting a tree. I was the tree, and thankfully, at the moment, there were no dogs.

"Good afternoon, sir," the nice-looking woman behind the front desk said as I stepped up to the polished wood counter.

I had cut inside the ropes like I knew what I was doing, and was actually feeling a little proud of myself at that moment. Avoiding front desk rope lines, combined with the flowing power of a casino around me, could sometimes be a heady experience. I savored the moment, then looked up at the woman who had greeted me.

Her smile actually included her eyes as she leaned forward a little. And what eyes they were. I had an out-of-body experience as I studied them.

Brown, large, and round, with the light over the front desk giving them a little twinkle. I could stare into those eyes forever, but I knew I shouldn't.

Yet I wanted to.

I knew I shouldn't.

Stare.

I shouldn't.

I floated there, arguing with myself, until I finally returned to my body and somehow managed to look at the rest of her.

She had long brown hair pulled back into a flowing ponytail, a smile that showed perfect teeth, and skin that was pleasantly tan. She wore the Horseshoe employee brown jacket and white blouse in such a way as to somehow make the dull outfit look sexy.

Of course, a woman with those eyes and that smile could make burlap look sexy as far as I was concerned, so my astute powers of perception on her uniform was more than likely skewed by my own interests.

"Checking in," I managed to say, even though my throat was suddenly dry.

"Here for the tournament?" she asked, her smile not fading.

"I am," I said. "That obvious?"

"Poker players do have a look about them," she said, laughing.

Her laugh was so fine, so perfectly tuned that it matched her smile, her eyes, her sexy look. The Horseshoe sure had a way of greeting a poker player. I wanted to stand on the counter, shout "Poker Boy is here to save you!" and jump her right there.

I refrained, but I had no doubt I was in love.

Actually, more accurately, lust.

I was in lust with Miss Brown-eyes behind the front desk. Nothing unusual, but very enjoyable.

It was good to be back in a casino.

"Your name, sir?" the beautiful woman—who I shall forever think of as Brown-eyes until I learned her name—asked.

She stood in a non-threatening manner behind the front desk of the Horseshoe Casino and Hotel, her fingers poised over the keyboard of her computer. I would have much rather had those fingers poised over me, but since she was about to type my name with those wonderful hands, I couldn't complain too much.

"Conway Moore," I said, giving her one of the fake names I had been using since I had become Poker Boy.

Her fingers stroked my name into her computer, her head nodding slightly.

I watched, mesmerized as her hands worked.

I often got mesmerized by a woman's hands. It only becomes a problem when a woman is playing with her chips in a poker game. I then have to force myself to stare down at my own chips at that point, or into the eyes of the other players to break the spell.

I would have loved to have told this woman behind the desk that my name was Poker Boy, but Poker Boy wasn't the name I had made the reservation under, so it would have just confused the issue.

Poker Boy was my superhero name, and Conway Moore was the other part of my superhero name, used when I needed to do regular world things like check into a hotel, sign into a poker tournament, rent a car, that sort of thing.

Actually, Conway Moore wasn't the name I was born with. I had known Poker Boy was going to need a secret identity to get by in the world. Conway seemed like a good name. Conway was also a character thought up by James Hilton in his novel *Lost Horizons*. I liked the book, so I borrowed the name for my secret identity.

At first, I thought about just using Conway as both my first and last names, then the last name of Moore came from a poker game like a hundred dollar bill laying in the parking lot.

Shortly after I became Poker Boy, some guy in a ten-twenty hold-em game accused me of never getting enough of his money. I don't remember what casino I was in, but I do remember that he said that all I wanted was more and more. I had to agree, since he was one of the worst poker players ever to flash a large roll of bills in front of me. As long as he sat there at the table and pulled out more bills, I sat there and took his money. Thus was the nature of poker.

And besides, a superhero had to eat.

On the way back to my room hours later, I kept thinking about how he just repeated "More and more and more." I decided that would be my last name. I changed the spelling of "more" to Moore to make it seem name-like. And thus, my secret identity of Conway Moore was born, both from the heart of a literary novel and the sweat of a poker game.

Perfect secret identity for Poker Boy.

"Here is your key, Mr. Moore," the woman said, sliding the paper packet with the plastic key toward me. I reached for it and her hand brushed mine.

I saw stars!

I saw the gambling gods!

I saw a royal flush against four aces, all in that order.

"I hope you have a good stay," she said. "And good luck in the tournaments."

Her smile was in full force, her wonderful eyes controlling me like a well-trained seal that could bark and balance a ball on its nose on command.

"Thank you," I managed to say without barking or balancing a ball.

Then I turned and tripped over my luggage.

Somehow, I managed to miss getting tangled in the front desk rope maze as I fell.

That floor may have been carpeted, and I may be a superhero, but it was still hard, and it still hurt.

"Are you all right, Mr. Moore?" she asked, a frown of worry crossing her beautiful face, making it beautiful in a different way. She leaned over the desk and looked down at me like an angel, the light behind her head giving her a halo.

I thought of lying there, staring at her until she floated over to help me up, then I thought better of it.

I sprang to my feet.

"I'm fine," I said, pretending to laugh it off.

I had heard that superheroes always spring back to their feet when knocked down, and I sure didn't want to be an exception to the rule in the superhero world, even when the fall was caused by my inability to not be consumed by a pretty woman.

That, and poorly placed luggage.

Every superhero has his weak spot. Superman has Krytonite, Poker Boy has pretty women. Especially pretty women with big, brown eyes who can make a plain hotel uniform look sexy.

Luckily, I took the fall while in my secret identity of Conway Moore. Conway Moore had far less to lose than Poker Boy.

The pretty woman behind the desk watched me, trying not to laugh, as I rounded up my kicked luggage.

"Thanks," I said, finally getting myself together.

"You're welcome," she said.

Her smile was different than the one she had greeted me with. I might have been only imagining it, which was very possible, but I think I felt in that smile amusement, maybe attached to a little fondness.

I turned and headed for the elevator. If I knew what was good for me, Poker Boy and his alter ego, Conway Moore, would stay very far away from that front desk area.

Yeah, right. And that was going to happen.

♦ 2 ♦

A BEAUTIFUL WOMAN
AND TROUBLE IS FOUND

I HAD LEFT MY LUGGAGE in my room, taken a quick nap, and then headed upstairs to get a great steak dinner. Now I was on the way to the tournament, the World Series of Poker, something I looked forward to every year. I had just gotten off the elevator on the second floor and turned to go to the tournament registration, when I saw my first dog of the trip.

Now, understand, as Poker Boy, I often end up saving dogs as well as people. In fact, it's a rare adventure that I don't save at least one dog.

The dog facing me looked like a mix between a golden retriever and a lab, although I wouldn't swear to either being in there. It was a beautiful dog, clearly well-kept and its longish golden hair was brushed regularly.

It was sitting next to a wall, watching everything around it with big, brown eyes. I was having a brown-eyed sort of day. Brown-eyed woman behind the counter, now a brown-eyed dog.

I didn't take it as a sign, but maybe I should have.

There was one of those seeing-eye walker contraptions on the dog's back, with a handle that was held by a very pretty woman wearing dark glasses. She leaned against the wall as if the wallpaper was giving her strength.

I had heard of stranger things giving people strength, but not many. Actually, I doubted the wallpaper was helping her at all, since it was a floral pattern that had faded over the years.

Since she was wearing dark glasses inside the hotel, it meant she was either a poker player, or blind, and from the looks of the dog sitting beside her, I would bet on her being blind, or at least vision impaired, as they liked to say this last decade or so.

I hesitated in my walk toward the poker tournament and studied her. She was beautiful, in sort of a Midwest, take-her-home-to-meet-the-mother way. Her face was scrubbed, no make-up and her light brown hair was combed and pulled back. She had on black slacks that were well-pressed, and a white blouse which showed just a hint of the white bra under it.

And there was something wrong with her.

I stopped and stepped out of the main flow of traffic in the hallway, letting two of the better known poker columnists walk past me talking about a player I didn't know.

With tournament poker growing so fast, there were a lot of players I didn't know these days.

I studied the woman standing beside her dog. There was something about her that needed help. I would have to use one of Poker Boy's superpowers to find out.

Raising my arm like I was trying to fix something caught in the long hair on my neck, I pulled slightly while staring at her.

Pulling on my own hair was one of my ways of triggering one of my superpowers. That, and focus.

Mostly focus. I really didn't need the hair-pulling part, but it acted like a trigger for me and helped. I was still fairly new at all this and any trick helped.

After a moment of tugging on my hair, the hallway, the carpet, the other people moving about seemed to vanish as everything I could see narrowed down on the woman and my Extra-Vigilant-Vision took over.

I had always wished as a young man to have Superman's X-Ray vision. What teenage boy didn't? What fun it would have been to see into women's locker rooms, see through women's dresses, see through walls to know when your mom was coming so that you could stop masturbating because you were staring into the neighbor's house watching the girl next door take a bath.

Oh, what fun it would have been to have that superpower as a teenaged boy.

So when I grew up and became Poker Boy, I thought I might get lucky and manage X-Ray vision, but instead all I could do was Extra-Vigilant-Vision, which was the ability to look at something very closely. I couldn't see through anything, but as an adult and a poker player, I had come to realize this was almost as good.

Especially at a poker table when I was trying to discover if a player was bluffing. All I had to do was stare at the player and with my Extra-Vigilant Vision I would be able to see clearly if they were worried, or confident, and then make my bet accordingly.

The woman under my special superpower vision gave me a lot of clues quickly that something was very wrong with her. She was breathing faster than normal, her bra pushing up against the fine fabric of her white blouse. I could almost see the pores in her skin, which looked pale, as if not getting enough blood. It was also clear that she might start perspiring at any moment.

Her head moved back and forth, as if trying to listen to everything around her at once. Her hand grasped the dog leader like it was a life-line tossed to someone drowning.

She looked scared and very worried.

Suddenly another superpower kicked in, my Ultra-Intuition Power shouted at me, *She's lost. Or has lost something.*

Actually that power doesn't shout, it sort of echoes, like a deep voice coming up from a canyon into my mind. Imagine the deepest base singer in the Temptations saying to me from a deep, dark hole in the ground. *She's lost-t-t-t-t-t* and you'll have the idea.

When two of my superpowers start working at the same time, I'm really hard to beat at a poker table. And in real life. This woman and her dog needed my help. That much was clear.

I dropped out of Extra-Vigilant Vision so I could see if anyone else was around, then stepped toward her. She turned, as if she knew I was coming at her, even though my shoes had made no sound on the carpet of the hallway.

When a person was blind, the other senses kicked in, often making up for the lost sense. Since she knew I was coming and I hadn't made a sound, I figured she might have something similar to my Big Nose Super-Sniffing Power. I hadn't needed to use that superpower very often, but twice so far it had saved the day.

"Excuse me," I said before I got very close to her, "you look like you might need some help?"

For an instant panic seemed to flash over her face, then she got herself under control and asked, "Do you work here?"

A logical question under the circumstances.

"Actually, no," I said, stopping far enough away so that I would give no threatening signs to either her, or her dog, who was looking up at me with a worried look in those big, brown eyes.

"I'm just here to play in the tournament. My name's Conway, and I know my way around this old hotel pretty well. It's a confusing maze, even on the best of days. I'd be glad to help you if you need it."

"Actually," she said, smiling at me, her face relaxing a little under her dark glasses, "I know exactly where I am. But thank you."

"Then can I help you find whatever it is that you've lost?" I asked.

I knew my Ultra-Intuition Power had not been wrong. If she knew where she was, then her problem was that she had lost something else.

My question made her jerk, and again her skin paled slightly, even noticeably without my vision super-power in use.

"How did you know I am looking for someone?"

I laughed. "How did you know I was coming toward you when you couldn't hear me?"

She thought for a moment, then laughed with me. "Top sirloin, rare."

I was impressed.

"So I assume," I said, pressing on with her problem, "that you have tried all the regular methods, such as having this person paged? Having an employee check the tournament room? And so on."

Modern casinos, and even old ones like the Horseshoe, are extremely easy to get lost in. And without clocks anywhere, and the focus on money and games, time can seem to vanish. People being lost in a casino is a common problem, and usually not one that would require Poker Boy's help.

But I knew, without a doubt, and from my Ultra-Intuition Power, that this woman needed me.

"I have," she said, nodding. "A number of times, actually. They are starting to think I am nuts."

"Who is missing?" I asked.

Sometimes the best power a superhero has was to simply ask the right questions and then listen very carefully to the answer.

"My husband," she said, a look of caring and concern on her face.

I could tell, by my heightened ability as a poker player and not as Poker Boy, that she really loved her husband. This wasn't the old tired cliché of the married couple coming to Las Vegas and the husband dumping the blind wife and running off with a Keno girl.

No, this guy was really missing.

"When was the last time you were with him?" I asked.

"We were eating lunch at the café downstairs, the one in the basement."

I knew the place well. It too had the feel of an old supper club, but it had been remodeled with the wood posts and low ceilings to look a little like a Carnegie library with tables. The waiters wore short, white aprons over black pants and white shirts and always seemed extra busy, even at times there was almost no one in the place. Every time I ate there I always felt as if I should order something more with my omelet, just to make it worth the waiter's time and energy.

"I've eaten there," I said to her. "So what happened?"

She took a deep breath, clearly blaming herself for what she was about to tell me.

"I wanted to sit and just finish my tea, so Ben, my husband, said he would just go out in front of the restaurant and play the bank of slots there. He said he'd come back in and get me in fifteen minutes."

"He never did," I said.

She nodded. "I sat there for an hour, then paid the bill by charging it to our room. I got a waiter to help me get out of the restaurant and up the stairs to the slot machines, thinking Ben had gotten wrapped up in winning and had forgotten about coming back for me. No one around the top of those stairs remembered seeing him."

My Ultra-Intuition Power was rumbling in the back of my brain, clearly almost ready to echo me a deep-voiced insight.

"I had him paged," she said, "and I had security look for him. About two hours after he vanished I went back to our room and waited until about an hour ago. I don't know what to do, to be honest with you."

"And I know the Vegas police won't help until a certain amount of time has gone by," I said.

Again she nodded. "It took me an hour on the phone to finally get that figured out."

My Ultra-Intuition superpower was still rumbling, but nothing was echoing forth from the depths just yet. I still needed a little more information.

"Did he say which bank of slots he was going up to play?"

She shrugged. "No, but he liked the really old slots. That's why he liked staying downtown instead of out on the strip."

Ghost slots!

My Ultra-Intuition shouted at me, the sound echoing around inside my head like my brain was missing.

"Ghost slots," I said out loud, not really meaning to.

"Ghost slots?" she asked.

"Nothing," I said. "Would you mind walking me down to the restaurant and showing me anything else you might remember."

She cocked her head sideways a little. "I don't even know you, Mr. Conway."

"Actually, the name is Conway Moore," I said. "And I think you do know me. And could use my help."

"Are you the police? Or a detective?"

"Neither," I said. "Just a person who helps when someone needs help."

She reached out slowly and touched my arm, then my shoulder, then ran her hand over my face, noting my black hat, lack of facial hair, and black leather coat that was part of my superhero uniform I always wear.

The hat was a Fedora-style and combined with my coat, it seemed to focus my energy when in a casino.

Then she nodded. "You're right, I do need your help. And I would be willing to pay for it."

I laughed. "Payment is not necessary. I make my money playing poker, and that's good enough for me. Just say thank you when we find Ben."

Again she sort of stood there, clearly running all her emotions and senses about me over in her mind. Could she trust me? Should she trust me? Did she have any better options at the moment?

Under normal circumstances, this woman would never accept help from some strange man. But Poker Boy has a way of putting people at ease, making them feel as if they know me, without ever really knowing anything about me. I am convinced it is one of the superpowers that goes along with the job, but I couldn't come up with a decent name for it.

And I had tried. Ultra-Acceptance Power didn't feel right. Come-to-me-for-help Power didn't do it either. For a time I had called it my Trust-Me Superpower, but that sort of went away as any bad name does.

Plus, I couldn't call it up at will. It was sort of just there.

"Okay, Mr. Conway Moore," she said. "I'll thank you now for your help, and after we find Ben."

"Deal," I said. It seemed my unnamed, superpower worked even on the blind.

She stuck out her hand and I grasped the warm, firm grip. "Deal," she said. "And by the way, my name is Samantha. And this is Sue."

She bent down slightly and patted the top of the beautiful golden-haired dog.

"Sue and Samantha MacDuff," the woman added.

"Nice meeting you both," I said.

I am convinced we were both glad I didn't ask the obvious question about why anyone would name a dog Sue.

And it took every bit of super will-power I had to not say, when she turned toward the elevator, pulling her dog around, "Lead on MacDuff."

I didn't say it, but I wanted to.

◆◆ 3 ◆◆

A SIDEKICK JOINS THE FUN

SAMANTHA, SUE, AND I wound our way through the gaming tables and slot machines until we were near the front of the cafe. I maneuvered us into an area out of the way so that Samantha would have a wall to lean against.

As I had expected, there were no older-looking slots anywhere near the front of the restaurant. In fact, I had been watching for older slots since we got to the main casino floor, and hadn't seen any.

"Okay, what does your husband look like?" I asked, just a fraction of a second before I realized I was asking that question of a blind woman. "Oh, sorry."

She laughed and patted my arm. "It's all right. I've only been blind the last eight years of my life. And I was already married to Ben before this happened."

"Okay," I said, again restraining from asking about how she had become blind. Instead I focused on the task at hand. "So anything you can tell me would help. Height, hair color, balding or not? And do you know what he was wearing this morning? That sort of thing."

She nodded, turning her head slightly to listen as a machine half the room away released a flood of coins, one right after the other into a tray, banging as a loud alarm went off. Casinos always wanted to draw attention to any time they gave away money, but never when they took it. Just good business sense. But any customer with any common sense knew they didn't build those multi-billion dollar resorts out on the Strip by giving away too much money.

"Ben stands five-foot-ten," Samantha said, "weighs about one hundred and seventy, and keeps himself in good shape. He has thinning brown hair, with a hairline that has started to recede slightly. He was wearing tan slacks, a brown golf shirt, and deck shoes this morning."

"Perfect," I said. "Will you be all right standing here for a few minutes while I look around?"

"I'll be fine," she said.

I touched her arm lightly, then turned away, heading down the flight of stairs in to the restaurant. I had to check a few things before I went any farther in helping her.

A number of times I have had people come to me for help who were actually in no need of help. I wish I had a superpower that could tell when someone was lying or not. But I didn't, so I had to rely on the old fashioned way, asking questions like a detective would. And even though I had approached her, and everything about her story made sense, I still had to check.

I found the restaurant manager and within a few seconds confirmed the woman's story. She and a guy had been having breakfast, he left her after they had finished, and she seemed to wait for him for an hour before paying and asking to be helped up the stairs.

That was all the information I needed. That, combined with my Ultra-Intuition Power confirmed for me she was telling me the truth.

"Any luck?" she asked me before I got within ten feet of her. Clearly this woman's hearing was fantastic, or the steak I had eaten for dinner was still with me.

"I didn't see him anywhere," I said. "And there are no older slot machines anywhere near here."

"Really?" she asked, seemingly surprised. "When I came up to the top of the stairs after waiting, the manager asked a few of the people in the area if they had seen Ben. I heard one of them tell him they thought they had seen him playing the old Saturn Slots near the stairs."

I glanced at the staircase. No Saturn Slots anywhere to be seen. Just a half dozen video poker games and some newer Monopoly machines. I didn't want to think about the chance those Saturn Slots had been ghost slots.

"Let's go get some more information." I took her gently by the arm and led her, and her dog Sue, through the tight rows of slots, past the gaming tables, and toward the front desk.

I was hoping the woman with the big brown eyes would be behind the main desk, and I was in luck. She looked up at me, smiled fondly, and for an instant I was lost again.

But the feeling only lasted an instant, since I wasn't just Conway Moore checking in, I was Poker Boy, helping a woman and her dog. Superhero duties come first, even over lust.

The woman with brown eyes looked over at the blind woman and frowned, a worried look crossing that beautiful face. "Mrs. MacDuff, have you found your husband yet?"

"I'm afraid not," Samantha said.

Clearly this woman had been involved with the paging that Samantha had done earlier.

"So what can I do to help?" the woman asked, glancing at me.

I knew right then that this brown-eyed employee would be a valuable assistant. I'm not sure which of my powers told me that, but I was convinced.

"I'm hoping we could get your help, or someone's help in the back office," I said, smiling at her and putting on my best Poker Boy charm. "We need to find out where a certain bank of slots are in the casino. Or if they are still here."

"And that would help Mrs. MacDuff find her husband?"

"It might," I said. "It's the only bit of information we have to work with at the moment.

I didn't want to get into my theory that Ben might have been taken by ghost slots. Neither of these women, or Sue the dog for that matter, would believe me. At least not yet. And I didn't want to make myself look like a fool without some proof to back up my theory.

The woman with the brown eyes held my gaze for a long moment, as if she knew what I was thinking, then she nodded. "All right."

She glanced over at a man dressed in the same uniform she was. "Dan, I'm going to help these folks for a few minutes, then head for home."

Dan only nodded and kept typing something into a computer in front of him. Clearly this woman was about to get off for the night. Normally, if I wasn't working on a case, that might have interested me. Now that part of my interest would have to wait for another time.

The woman indicated that we should move to a heavy-looking wood door off one side of the main desk. She led us inside and down a hallway to a room with big desks. I could tell at a glance that this office had been in use for the same function for a lot of years, and had more than likely been missed in the big remodeling back in the eighties and nineties.

In all my years before becoming a superhero, I hadn't managed to get behind the scenes once in a hotel or casino. But since becoming Poker Boy, it seemed I did a lot of wandering around in offices and secure areas that most normal folk didn't even know existed.

The only man in the room stood immediately as we entered. "What's going on, Patty?"

Now I knew the brown-eyed desk clerk's name. It fit her, actually.

"This is Mrs. MacDuff," Patty said, indicating Samantha. "And Mr. Moore. This is our Manager on Duty, Bob Silvers."

Bob's stern look immediately melted when he heard Samantha's name. "No luck finding your husband yet?"

Samantha shook her head. "Mr. Moore is helping me. It's still too early to get the police involved."

"So what can we do to help?" Bob asked, glancing at me, then back at Samantha.

I took the lead, using my nicest, most convincing voice. "Two things, actually," I said. "First off, would it be possible to look up where a bank of slot machines were in this casino?"

Bob sort of jerked, clearly catching my use of past tense. He turned to stare at me. "You don't think that—."

Clearly Bob had heard of ghost slots. It sometimes surprised me how many people in Vegas had. But I didn't want him blurting that out just yet, so I interrupted him.

"I don't know what to think just yet," I said. "But if we know where the slots that Ben MacDuff was seen playing are located, we might be able to find something on a surveillance camera that would tell us what happened."

He glanced at the frowning face of Samantha, and then at the worried face of Patty, and nodded. Without another word, he turned back to his desk and grabbed two badges that said "Guest" on them in big red letters.

"Wear these," Bob said. "Patty will help you look up the information you need. If you don't mind staying a little after your shift, Patty?"

"Not at all," she said, smiling at me as she helped hook Samantha's guest pass on her white blouse.

And with that look, I knew that Poker Boy had found his sidekick. I had no doubt that Patty had her own share of superpowers to bring to the case of the missing MacDuff. With Patty, the fun part was going to be figuring out what those powers might be. I would bet that most of them were hooked into those big, brown eyes.

And the ability to make a hotel uniform look sexy.

•◆ 4 ◆•

ONE OFFICE, NO WINDOWS, NO ESCAPE

PATTY LED ME, Samantha, and her dog, Sue, down a well-lit back hallway of the Horseshoe Hotel and Casino to a large file room.

The place was windowless and had a few library-like tables in the center, with old file cabinets all around the outside of the room. A number of computers filled smaller work desks at different spots around the room, and each computer had a stack of files beside it. There was no one in the room when we got there, which actually relieved me.

Working in a room like this was my worst nightmare. The place smelled of old paper and bad air-conditioning, and I had a hard time imagining working in such a room for eight hours a day.

I had no doubt that if I tried to work regularly in there, even just a few hours a day, the plain painted walls and pictures of old Vegas taken back in the fifties would soon close in, smashing me like a fly between the pages of a book. I would be nothing more than a blood and guts splatter over the file cabinets, my very essence merging with the dull paint and old photos.

Luckily, I had learned how to play poker for a living and became Poker Boy so I didn't have to sit very often in such dull rooms.

"We're trying to get all of the most important old information entered into the computer system," Patty said. "But it's taking time, and with a casino this old it's a difficult task at best. There's a lot of information and people only work on it during slow times."

"And with the World Series of Poker starting up, this isn't a slow time," I said.

"Far from it," Patty said, laughing as she got Samantha seated at a table with Sue sitting at her feet. Then Patty sat down at one of the computers and keyed in the words "Saturn Slots" as I watched over her shoulder, trying to focus on her and what she was doing instead of the room around me.

"Nothing," she said, shaking her wonderful, soft-looking hair as the screen came up blank. "I was afraid of that. These computer records only go back ten years on slots."

"And no Saturn Slots during that time?" I asked. "Or anything with the name Saturn?"

"Nothing," Patty said.

"So we have to go back farther by hand," I said, "if there are records for that."

"There are," Patty said.

I was amazed. Hundreds of thousands of slot machines must have come through this casino over the years. Clearly the state gambling board, or the IRS, made them keep track of all of them. Sometimes all the stupid regulations of "Big Brother" came in handy.

Behind us Samantha said, "But I don't understand why we're looking for slot machines that are that old. Ben just disappeared today."

"I know," I said, "but you did say you overheard someone saying they thought they saw him playing the Saturn Slots. Right?"

She nodded. "But if slots like that haven't been in this casino for ten years, how could he have been playing them. I guess I just don't—"

Patty interrupted. "We're just trying to eliminate some things. It won't take too long, I promise."

Samantha said nothing more, but I could tell she was very confused.

I certainly didn't add in anything. The idea of there being such a thing as ghost slots was crazy, yet Patty and I, without actually saying anything to each other, were both worried that ghost slots had gotten Samantha's husband. We just didn't want to tell Samantha that theory without some proof.

Hell, I didn't even want to talk with Patty about it.

Patty stood and moved across the room to a file cabinet. I followed like a puppy on a leash, enjoying my time close to her. I had picked up a couple of details about Patty since our hike into the back room depths of the Horseshoe Casino. First off, she smelled wonderful, like a raspberry bush in full bloom. Across the front desk I hadn't had a chance to notice that.

Second, she had a mole on her neck that flashed in and out of sight under her hair, sort of teasing me to come closer. I'm not saying I have a thing about moles. There was nothing sexual or kinky about a parasite growing on a human, but that said, I sure hoped me and that mole would get a lot closer over time.

I made myself stop staring at her mole as she pulled open the second drawer of the old metal cabinet and thumbed quickly through some files.

The moment I stopped staring at the mole, the room started to close in again, so I gladly went back to my focus on her neck while she worked.

"Here it is," she said as she pulled out a thin file. "Saturn Slots. There were four of them in one bank." She turned and put the file on the top of the cabinet before opening it for both of us to see.

A colorful ball in the image of Saturn, tipped slightly to one side, dominated the area above the slots. The planet's rings extended even higher into the air and also down, seemingly through a couple of the slot machines. It was a fine piece of old slot craftsmanship.

Most people don't know that the graphics and design that goes into slot machines has become almost an art form over the years. Casinos and slot machine companies have spent millions trying to figure out what attracts a player to a certain slot machine. The design, the playability, the graphics, the colors, the shapes of the box, the payouts, all have to combine to form something that is not only fun, but is easy to play, yet challenging enough to hold interest.

I know I considered slot design an art form, but I doubted we would be seeing slot machines in any art galleries anytime soon, which was a crime. Think about it. A gallery patron could enjoy the art show, and all that caché that went along with being an art snob, while at the same time playing a slot machine, with the art gallery taking a cut of the profits, of course.

I stared at the picture. All four Saturn Slots were the old-fashioned pull handle type, and all four looked old, like they had had some use by the time they reached the Horseshoe. On top of that, they were nickel machines. You didn't see many of those any more that weren't electronic and allowed a person to play twenty nickels at a time.

"Sixteen years," Patty said. One of her beautiful fingers pointed at a date. "We took them out sixteen years ago, after five years of play."

"Who leased them?" I asked, "Or who were they sold to when you got rid of them?"

In Vegas, and in many other places, some slot machines are owned and serviced by companies that are not affiliated with any one casino. Often, the machines are just leased to the casino. This is happening a lot with the new licensing of such media products as *Monopoly Games*, *The Adams Family*, and so on. I didn't know if the Horseshoe leased or bought their own machines. My hunch was they did both.

"Valley Slots," Patty said, studying the paper in front of her. "We leased them."

"Damn," I said. "Valley Slots has been out of business for a good ten years. I think Standard bought part of their assets."

Patty nodded. "I seem to remember something about that."

"Does it say where these slots were on the floor sixteen years ago?"

"Not from the records," Patty said. She pointed to the picture. "But from the looks of that, they were set up just outside the restaurant."

I looked closer. She was right. The distinctive wooden railing that led down into the basement restaurant was clearly visible to one side of the slots. Luckily, when they had done the remodeling of the casino and restaurants, they had decided to go back to how it had looked. Sometimes retrograde designs saved time and money, and in this case it helped us.

"Well," I said, turning to Samantha, "we found where the slots were."

"Sixteen years ago," Samantha said, her disgust not well hidden in the tone of her voice.

"Would you know exactly what time Ben left the restaurant?" Patty asked.

"Just after one," Samantha said. "We went down for lunch at noon, and they were a little slow. I remember checking my watch and it was one just a few minutes before he left."

Patty moved over to a phone sitting beside the door and dialed a five-digit number.

I sat down beside Samantha at the table and patted her arm. Sue moved around under the edge of the table a little to nudge against my leg, clearly thanking me in dog language. Either that or she wanted to be petted. I knew better than to pet a dog trained for seeing-eye work, so I refrained.

Around me, the room closed in even more. I was sweating and I wanted to take off my Poker Boy leather coat and special hat, but I knew better. We needed to do this research and get out of here before Poker Boy, superhero, lost it and went screaming down the hall.

"Steward, this is Patty in the file room. I need you to pull up the security tape for the area outside the restaurant stairs. From one this afternoon to one-ten. Can you feed it to me in here?"

She listened for a moment, then said, "Yeah, include the stairs. And set it to replay a few times would you? Thanks." Then she hung up.

"We're going to know more in a minute," she said.

"Thank you both for all your help," Samantha said.

"Thank us after we find out what happened to Ben," Patty said. She moved over to a security monitor sitting on the top of a file cabinet against one wall. She clicked it on to show a blank screen.

I patted Samantha's arm and stood to join Patty and her wonderful raspberry smell and attractive mole. The mole wasn't visible at the moment, but the smell lured me closer like a flower's nectar to a bee who couldn't report back to the hive without filling a quota.

"It's going to take Steward a few seconds to get the tape up," Patty said. "Luckily, we upgraded our entire security system this last winter. It's now state of the art."

I could feel my stomach twisting. I had no idea if we were actually going to see, on tape, evidence of ghost slots taking a man. If so, we were going to be the only people to ever see this tape, of that much I was certain. It would be destroyed at once.

There was no casino on the planet that wanted the press release about slot machines kidnapping customers. And besides, even with a tape, who would believe it. If what we thought had happened showed up on this tape, another tape, of say a quiet time ten minutes before, would replace it, all time-coded to look perfect, of course.

And no one would dare say anything different.

That was why the general public didn't know about ghost slot machines, or a dozen other strange things that went on in Las Vegas. It just wasn't good for business. But anyone who was in Vegas for any amount of time, working or playing like I did, heard about these things.

Suddenly the screen flicked to life. It was the image of the stairs down into the restaurant, and the slots around the top of the stairs, all shown from a camera in the ceiling. A time code was running on the bottom.

There was no sign of any Saturn Slots in their old location. The slots that occupied that spot now were newer Monopoly machines.

An older couple came up the stairs, turning and heading for the door out into the heat. A moment later a man started up the stairs.

"That's him," I said.

"You see Ben?" Samantha asked.

"He's on the security tape," I said. "Coming out of the restaurant."

Patty pointed to the area where the Monopoly slots had been a moment before. Now the Saturn Slots sat there, the image of the ringed planet in full neon, the lights blinking.

"Oh, shit," I said softly.

Ben reached the top of the stairs, turned and moved over in front of the bank of Saturn Slots, fishing in his pocket for change as he went. The old machines didn't take bills, but he dug a role of nickels out of his pocket.

Then he sat down into one of the chairs attached to the front of the Saturn Slots, dropped a coin into the slot, and reached for the handle.

As he pulled it he seemed to freeze.

The old wheels on the slots spun, but from the angle of the camera, I couldn't see what they showed.

Ben seemed to shake for a moment, his hand still holding the arm of the machine.

A moment later the Saturn Slots faded away, taking Ben with them.

I somehow managed to take a deep breath, staring at what were normal, modern slots where the Saturn Slots had been a moment before.

"I never thought I'd ever see it happen," Patty said, her voice hushed.

"What?" Samantha demanded from where she sat at the table.

A moment later the phone rang as the tape cut off, not repeating as Patty had asked.

Patty picked up the phone and listened. Then she said, "I understand."

She hung the phone up slowly before turning off the monitor.

"We never saw that?" I asked.

"We never saw that," she said.

"Would one of you please tell me what just happened?" Samantha demanded. "Do you know where Ben is?"

The silence in the room got so loud I thought the door might burst outward from the pressure.

Patty and I just stood there, staring at the blind woman and her dog, Sue. How do you tell someone her husband was kidnapped by a gang of old nickel slot machines?

How do you tell someone that one of the urban myths of Vegas was true, and had just been caught on film, which was being destroyed as we stood there letting the silence get louder and louder.

How does anyone tell a wife that her husband had been taken by ghost machines, and we had no idea to where, or to when, for that matter?

I knew for a fact there just wasn't an easy way.

So instead, I changed the subject. I have learned over the years that changing the subject with a woman in the middle of a serious discussion often only makes matters worse, but at the moment it was the only thing I could think to do.

I turned to Patty. "Have you had dinner?" I knew this was a strange way to get a first date, but at this point, any date was better than none.

Besides thinking of the date and getting closer to that mole, I had to get us all out of the room, which was more than likely heavily monitored, before we could have any discussion about what we had seen.

And I had to get myself out before I melted into a puddle of Poker Boy fluids that would surely stain the floor. The walls were getting *really* tight.

Patty glanced at me, puzzled. Then she realized what I was doing. Or at least part of what I was doing. I hope she didn't know about my desire to get closer to the mole on her neck.

"No, I haven't. And I'm hungry."

"How about you, Samantha?" I asked.

"I don't think I could eat," she said. "I just want to know what happened to Ben."

"Well, you're going to need to eat," I said, making my voice sound as upbeat as I could without making it sound like a game show host. "To keep your strength up to help us find Ben. We'll talk about all this over food, I promise."

Again the silence filled the room, making the walls close in even faster. This room was bad enough all by itself for me, but silence was making it torture. We needed to get out of here.

Seconds ticked past.

I started sweating. Or more likely I noticed I again that I was sweating.

Patty and I just stood there, Sidekick and Superhero, staring at the woman we were supposed to be trying to help. But we needed to get out of this room, and maybe out of the casino for the coming discussion.

More seconds ticked past as a blind woman faced us with sun-glassed-covered eyes.

I thought about putting out my arms and trying to hold the walls back, but I knew that wouldn't work any more than it worked in the first Star Wars movie. I was in the trash-compactor of offices and there was no robot to throw a switch to save me.

More seconds.

Not even the wonderful raspberry smell of Patty kept me from sweating even more. I doubted even a close-up visit to the mole would save me at this point.

The walls really were closing in.

Honest.

Finally, Samantha pushed herself to her feet, moving to get Sue into position. "I suppose I'm not going to find out what you saw while we're in here. So lead me to food."

I barely made it through the door seconds before those walls smashed me into brainless pulp and trapped me in a windowless of-fice, working a filing and data-entry job the rest of my life.

It had been close.

I had almost ended up living my worst nightmare. I was shaking as I went down the hall, forcing myself to not run.

I'm a superhero who helps people, rescues dogs, and plays poker for a living. I never said things didn't scare me.

But it had been worth the risk. We knew what had happened to Ben, and I had a dinner date with Patty.

·•♦ 5 ♦•·

ADDICTION

PATTY SEEMED TO KNOW where she wanted to go, so I followed along as she took Samantha's arm and expertly got her and her dog Sue from the back rooms, through the slots, and out one of the many doors of the Horseshoe Casino and Hotel.

We emerged onto what used to be called "Glitter Gulch" back in the days when train passengers got off the train a few blocks away and faced a street lined with blazing lights and signs.

Vegas Vic, a two-story tall, rail-thin, neon cowboy still looked over Frontier Street, just as he did back in the forties. He had a cigarette hanging from his mouth like a bad movie cliche, and a thumb that pointed toward who knew where.

In the old days, his thumb was meant to direct customers to the Pioneer Club. I suppose a two-story tall cowboy with a butt hanging out of his mouth was an attraction. I never saw him as that. I thought of him more as a landmark of downtown Vegas, a symbol, if you will, of the merging of the cowboy west with the neon lights of gambling, punctuated by the threat of dying from cancer.

A perfect Las Vegas icon.

During the sixties, Glitter Gulch had become more like a classic skid row as the strip casinos miles away became more popular. Back then the bums hung out on the street corners, the casinos didn't have the money to fix much of anything, and only the gamblers who were into grinding out each buck went downtown. Even with the Horseshoe starting the World Series of Poker back in the early seventies, I didn't want to go down there. There was just too much fun to be had out on the strip.

Things for downtown Las Vegas started to change in the early 1980's as the city did everything it could to revive the downtown area. They even went so far as to turn a few blocks of Frontier Street into a pedestrian mall and cover it with a light show that was hard to match. I think I remember hearing there were about two and a half million bulbs in that canopy over those four city blocks, but I could be off by a few hundred thousand either way.

Now, with the casinos around the big downtown mall remodeled as much as the space would allow, the area had at least held steady for a few years. I sort of liked it more now than the strip, actually. It had a more personal feel about it than the big super casinos.

And it was only a few feet between casinos instead of dozens of football fields. And when you're walking on a hot evening, that's an important consideration.

The heat slapped at me as we stepped outside. Even though the sun was setting on the town that never slept, it was still damn hot. In the middle of the night in the summer it was known to stay above a hundred degrees here. It was too early in the year for that kind of really intense heat, but it was still hot outside.

Too hot for my tastes, but after my close call with office death, it felt good to be out under the darkening blue sky and millions of light bulbs.

Patty quickly got us across the mall area, around a corner, and into the wonderful coolness of a cafe tucked between a casino and the side of an office building. The place had the feel of a fake diner, with bright replicas of things from the fifties plastered all over the walls.

I doubted any place actually looked like this back in the fifties. This was just a twenty-first century version of what people thought diners looked like in 1955. I hope the history books recorded the decade more accurately than diners, or the country's kids were going to be really messed up.

However, what the tacky pictures of Elvis and poodle-skirts on the walls often meant was decent food and large portions. Monster portions, actually. A burger in a place with a bubbling jukebox (always a replica of a real bubblier) was extra big, with more fries than an Idaho potato field.

And God forbid you order a milkshake with your burger. Unless your body had a high tolerance for sugar and milk, don't order a milkshake in a place with fifties memorabilia on the walls. It will be so good you'll have to drink it all, and so big you'll regret doing it. So the safest course is just not order one.

Since I was still full from my wonderful steak, I ordered an iced tea and nothing more from a woman who looked like she might have actually been a waitress since the fifties. Her face had more ravines than the Grand Canyon and her lips were painted bright red, with a gloss that made them seem to extend off her face. Her bright blue eyeliner contrasted with her large black hair and pink waitress uniform with the name Madge clinging to the top of her large right breast.

Madge, chewing gum and without a word, took my drink order, Patty's order of a salad and diet coke, and Samantha's order of a cheese sandwich and coffee. Then she nodded to Sue and spoke for the first time. "I'll bring the dog a dish of water."

With a pop of her gum, she turned and headed for the kitchen.

My gaze followed her for a moment, wishing almost instantly I hadn't. My mind shouted, "Don't look!"

But habit wins, and even if I am a superhero, I am a male. I couldn't help myself, honest. I looked at Madge's ass moving under the tight skirt as she walked away. Her ass was large and sagged in places a woman's ass shouldn't sag. It was also clear that Madge wore bikini underwear under her pink uniform. Even through the uniform it looked like that underwear hurt.

I knew, without a doubt, the image of Marge's ass would haunt me for the rest of the World Series of Poker.

Madge walked past a row of sit-down video poker machines, the type seen everywhere in Nevada and many other states. An elderly woman sat at the second one, her big black purse beside her, her attention focused on the screen, her hand shaking every time she made a play.

She had thinning, gray hair done up in a type of bun, and was wearing an older-style long cloth coat that looked like it had seen better days back when Madge was young and could wear bikini underwear without shocking guys like me.

When you play live poker against other players in a poker room, or home game, skill is everything. You win what the other players and your comparative skill allow you to win. But poker machines are set to pay the house a given amount, called an edge, just like a slot machine. Sure, it might be set loose, meaning it will return to the player ninety-nine out of every one hundred bets made, but it still kept that one bet. And given enough time, those one bets built huge casinos.

Most video poker machines were not set that loose.

On a video poker machine, you could knock that edge down some by making good decisions, but you could never really beat the machines day in and day out, no matter what any book (written by a guy making money from writing a book) told you.

Studies have shown that of all the slot machines, for some reason, video poker was the most addictive. The theory was that it engaged the player more than just yanking on a crank, or pushing a button and watching wheels spin. And that engagement turned into a form of gambling addiction.

As I watched, the old woman reached into her big black purse, pulled out a ten-dollar bill, and fed it to the machine, which yanked it from her trembling fingers.

I had no idea what that woman's story was. She might be very rich and very lonely, and playing that machine was just her way of passing the time.

Or she might be playing a part of her retirement funds with that last bet, allowing herself only ten or twenty or thirty dollars in losses every time she played. She might have that kind of control. Most people did.

Or maybe that was food money she had just put in there.

Or money she had gotten from selling something she had owned for decades. Maybe she was one of the growing numbers of elderly that were addicted to the machines and unable to get away.

Or not want to get away.

For many people, playing the machines gave life reason, and hope, and excitement where there was none. It was a reason to get up in the morning, something to look forward to the next day. The excitement of the big wins made them feel alive for a short time.

Las Vegas (and every casino in the world) was full of men and women like that gray-haired woman sitting at that machine. They all played for their own varied reasons, just like I played live poker for mine.

But it was said that men and women like her created the ghost slots. Or at least so the theory goes. At some point in the past, I was sure that someone had spent weeks, or even years, playing the Saturn Slots, begging them, cussing at them, talking to them, pleading with them, day in and day out. Those slots had become a person's life, had given them both joy and misery.

Sometimes for months, sometimes for years, a person can pour his or her life force into a slot machine, until finally the time came when not only did the machine have all the person's money, but it held their entire being.

The numbers of people who died every year in Las Vegas playing slot machines was another well-kept secret, but it happened so often no casino thought much about it. There was always another live body to take the cold one's place.

But who were these people who died? No study I had ever seen had looked into it, but I was sure that most were just tourists who had heart attacks. But a few were regulars, local residents, gambling addicts who made one machine a part of their life, and of their death.

And in that death, when some person gave a slot machine everything they had, the theory was that the machine took on a life of its own.

But like any slot machine, it must be fed. Only ghost slots don't need money, they need more life.

I'm a superhero and I have no idea where my powers come from. Half the time I can't even figure out names for the powers I have. As a person given superhero powers to help others, I know that there are many strange things in this world. And having ghost slots was not beyond my belief system.

But I also understood that a person does not have to be kidnapped by a ghost slot to lose themselves, their lives, and their loved ones to a machine.

It happened all the time, all over the world.

As I watched the old woman with the big black purse, she pulled out another ten-dollar bill and the machine ate it like a hungry animal.

She didn't even seem to notice.

◆◆ *6* ◆◆
ANOTHER SUPERHERO

IT BECAME CLEAR, in very short order, before Madge even got back with our drinks, that Samantha was not going to believe Patty and me about what happened to her husband.

We tried to tell her, honest we did, but our story sounded wild and far-fetched, even to me. I couldn't blame her for not believing us. She was blind, hadn't seen anything, and now had two people she had just met telling her that they had seen her husband taken away by ghost slot machines, but that the tape they had seen it on had been destroyed.

Yeah, right.

It would be simpler for her to believe we were trying to pull a scam on her than the story we were telling her.

Madge delivered our drinks and turned away. I managed not to look at her ass, but the image of the first look was still with me clearly.

And it was when I was trying to push the image of Madge in tight bikini underwear out of my mind that I realized I knew how to get Samantha to believe Patty and me.

I needed the help of another superhero.

"You have a cell phone?" I asked Patty.

She looked at me with those big brown eyes questioning me, then nodded.

The silence in our booth was cut only by the sound of Elvis singing "Hound Dog" on the jukebox. Patty handed me the phone and I dialed a number I had memorized a few years back.

The voice on the other end said, "Yeah?"

"Screamer," I said. "I need your help."

"Where are you at, Poker Boy?" Screamer asked, recognizing my voice at once and not making me identify myself in front of the women.

"A diner down off the mall on Frontier. Across from the Horseshoe."

"Madge working tonight?" he asked.

"She is," I said.

"Whatever you do," Screamer said, "don't look at her ass."

"Too late," I said.

"No wonder you need my help," he said. "I'll be there in five."

And he hung up.

"Who is Screamer?" Patty asked as Samantha shook her head in clear disgust. I had no doubt that she was about to get up and just leave.

"Screamer is a guy named Toledo Moss. He's been a friend of mine for years."

"Toledo Moss?" Patty said. "The same guy who helps the cops all the time?"

"The same guy," I said. "He does that for free. Mostly, he makes his living working with casinos stopping thefts."

Actually, what I didn't want to tell either one of them, especially Samantha, was that Screamer had a superpower. He could take the image from one person's mind and transfer it into another person's mind. Such a superpower made him a very strong weapon in solving all kinds of cases, especially if there wasn't enough proof, or a body had been hidden.

Screamer could take the image of the crime from the suspected criminal and transfer it into the cop's mind, and then the cop would go out and find the evidence that would stand up in court.

I was sure that taking of thoughts like that had to be protected under the Constitution in some fashion or another, but I doubt the original framers had given superpowers any thought. Just to be safe, though, Screamer never ended up in court on any case he helped solve, and no one really claimed what he said he could do actually worked.

It just did, and the cops and casinos that hired him left that alone.

"So how is this guy going to help find Ben?" Samantha asked.

I didn't answer, or brush off her question, because at that point Madge brought the food. And by the time she had turned to go back into the kitchen, Screamer had pulled a chair up to the table so he was between Patty and Samantha.

Screamer looked to be about forty, had a smile on him that woman said was to die for, and could stop a truck with his intense, green-eyed gaze. As far as I knew, he had never married, and with his ability to get inside another person's head, I wondered how he even managed to get close to many people.

I know a lot of my superpowers did not have off switches, but at least my powers needed me to be near a Casino and have my coat on to work. I couldn't imagine what kind of mental screens he must have developed if his powers worked all the time.

"Toledo Moss," I said, "meet Patty from the Horseshoe, and Samantha MacDuff, a guest there."

Samantha extended her hand and Screamer took it, gently shaking it while saying, "Nice meeting you."

Then he added, "I'm sorry about your husband. We'll find him."

I nodded. It was always a real pleasure as a superhero to see another superhero at work.

Screamer turned and took Patty's hand.

"Patty Ledgerwood," she said, smiling.

I was smiling as well. I now had her full name.

"Nice meeting you," Screamer said, his eyes lighting up at her touch.

My eyes would light up at her touch as well. I just hope Screamer didn't fall in love with her mole. I sort of felt possessive over that small spot on her neck since it had helped save me from being killed in dull-office-land.

"You're father's Alvin Ledgerwood, from the Dunes?"

"He is," Patty said.

"Tell him I said hello next time you see him. I hope his retirement is going fine. I worked many a case with him."

"He loves the free time," Patty said, "but he misses the work."

So now I knew that Patty was not only strikingly beautiful, but she was from an old-time Vegas family. No wonder she knew about ghost slots.

He let go of Patty's hand and then looked at me. "I see we have a little problem explaining what happened to Ben."

"Could you help?" I asked.

"I'd love to," Screamer said.

He again took Patty's hand, smiling at her, then reached over with his other hand toward Samantha.

"Mrs. MacDuff," Screamer said, his voice level and contained, "I'm going to show you something that Patty and The Boy here saw."

Without giving her time to say a word, he touched her arm.

She froze, her head up as if she was seeing something through the blind eyes and dark glasses.

Then, just at about the same length of time it had taken me and Patty to watch the ghost slots appear and take Ben, Screamer pulled away from both women.

Samantha shuddered, then sort of got smaller. After a moment she asked, "How did you do that?"

"It's my special gift," Screamer said. "I just took what Patty saw on that monitor and put it in your mind. I don't have the ability to alter anything."

"It felt like I was standing inside her. I know what she was thinking and seeing and feeling."

Oh, I would have loved that, but I didn't say anything.

She sort of turned her head so that if she had vision, she would have been looking at Patty. "I feel as if I invaded you. I'm sorry"

"I don't mind," Patty said, reaching across the table and untouched food and patting Samantha's arm.

"What you saw happened exactly that way," Screamer said. "If you just think about it for a second, you'll know I'm right."

Samantha shook her head and sat there for a moment. "So you're telling me you believe what you just showed me? How do I know you're not all in some sort of scam?"

Screamer smiled at me, then turned to talk directly to Samantha. "Ghost slots are not a laughing matter, and not something to be discounted. Ben was taken by ghost slots, of that I have no doubt, and these two people sitting with you are good people. You've got the best trying to help you get your husband back."

I wanted to thank Screamer for the glowing endorsement, but again I stayed silent.

"I've worked with the police a number of times over the years," Screamer said, "and would be glad to give you some names to call to confirm who I am. And trust me, Patty here has family that has been around this town almost from its old mining days."

He stayed silent about me, which I think is just fine. It's hard to explain Poker Boy, and right now Samantha was dealing with believing ghost slots. One thing at a time.

"It's just so hard to believe this happened," Samantha said, shaking her head.

"It happened," Patty said. "It's the first time I've seen it on tape, but I've been hearing about it my entire life. With the security cameras in casinos, I'm sure a lot of people have seen it. It just wouldn't be good for a casino's business to let out that this happens."

"So where is Ben?" Samantha asked. "Where did those machines take him?"

There was a long moment of silence, then I said softly, "That's what we're going to find out."

"As soon as we eat," Screamer said, leaning back and indicating that Madge should come take his order.

Madge made it over and took Screamer's order for a burger and fries, hold the onions, and I added a piece of cherry pie, since enough time had gone by that I could fit dessert around that candle-lit steak.

I suggested that Samantha eat, since she was going to need her energy to help us find Ben, and with that push she did.

I sat back and sort of studied the group as Screamer kept the two women entertained with a story about Patty's dad and a guy who had figured out a way to rob a casino of a thousand a day.

Almost every one of my adventures had a team. Very seldom did I solve a case completely alone. And from the looks of it now, this adventure had its team. A blind woman and her dog, a beautiful woman sidekick and her mole, a superhero named Screamer, and me, Poker Boy.

Those ghost slots didn't stand a chance.

Assuming, of course, we could find them. Ghosts of anything were never easy to track.

··◆ *7* ◆··

WHAT NEXT?
ALWAYS A GOOD QUESTION

AFTER TOLEDO MOSS, a.k.a. Screamer, finished his burger and iced tea, he looked at me. "Well? What next?"

So far the conversation over eating had been on anything but Ben and ghost slots. We had talked about the hot weather for April, I told them about the cab driver, and Samantha even told us how she got Sue a few years back for a birthday present from Ben. But I knew we had to figure out what to do next, so while the others had been talking, I had been planning.

Sitting silently and thinking is what any good poker player is good at. In fact, in no-limit hold-em tournaments, where a player's entire buy-in could be lost in one dumb play, I liked to just toss all my hands away for the first half hour to an hour and just sit back and watch players. That way I knew how a player acted, what he was likely to do, before I went up against him with my money.

So even with the wonderful talk and Patty being so close, I still managed to do some thinking, and had an answer for Screamer.

"Can you talk to your contacts at some of the major casinos around town?" I asked Screamer. "See if there have been any report-ed sightings of Ben and the Saturn Slots this afternoon and evening."

He nodded and I faced Patty and those brown eyes. "Could you have the Horseshoe's security team keep a close watch on that loca-tion near the stairs where the slots took Ben. Maybe they like the place. If they come back, we want to know when and how often."

"They'll do it for me," she said.

"Good thinking, Poker Boy," Screamer said, nodding, his gaze on something not in this room. "See if we can spot a pattern, maybe figure out where the slots and Ben are going to show next."

"We can only hope," I said. "At least it's a place to start. Patty, any chance you might have tomorrow off?"

"I'll take it off," she said, smiling at me.

I kept my face and heart under control and managed to keep going. "Great, thanks. Would you help me do some research into Valley and Standard Slots. Valley owned the things during the time they were in the Horseshoe. I'm betting they are still stored somewhere."

"Good thinkin' again," Screamer said. "Two-sided attack. Always nice to work with you, Poker Boy. You always got a play." He stood and dropped too much money on the table for his meal.

"I'll also check my contacts at the police, see if anything else is going on. You staying at the Horseshoe?"

"I am," I said.

"I'll call you at seven in the morning," Screamer said.

He turned to my sidekick, Patty. "It was wonderful crawling around inside that beautiful head of yours."

Patty had the common sense to blush and say nothing at Screamer's beaming smile.

"Samantha," Screamer said to her, touching her arm gently. "Don't worry. We'll find Ben. Try to get some rest. Tomorrow's going to be a full day."

"I'll try," Samantha said.

"Thanks, Screamer," I said.

He nodded to me and turned and was out the door. The room almost felt empty without him. Only the three of us, Elvis on the jukebox, and Madge were left in the diner. Screamer had a real presence about him.

"I never thought I'd ever meet the infamous Toledo Moss," Patty said, still blushing. "I heard my dad talk about him for years. He's almost a legend around this town."

"He is at that," I said, laughing, not mentioning that he was a superhero as well.

Patty stared at me, those brown eyes digging into my very heart, lifting the lid, swishing the blood around. Luckily I am a poker player who has been stared-down by the best in the business. But it's one thing to stare into the eyes of a player trying to find out your cards, it was another to stare into Patty's big brown eyes. I hope she never took up poker.

"Yet Toledo Moss deferred to you," Patty said, smiling slightly. "Why do you think that is?"

I just hoped at that moment my reputation around Las Vegas wasn't as strong as Screamers, because he had let slip my Poker Boy name a couple of times, and if anyone would have heard of me, then I have no doubt Patty would have as well.

"I've got a few years on him is all," I said, smiling at her.

"Why did you call him Screamer?" Samantha asked, coming to my rescue before Patty managed to peal back every ounce of protection I had with those laser-brown eyes of hers.

"I'm not sure who started it," I said. "But I've heard two reasons why."

"I only heard one," Patty said. "I heard that with his special gift of getting inside people's heads he could put nightmares into a person's mind until they screamed for him to stop."

"That's one," I said, smiling at Patty. "He did that for the cops on a serial murder case about fifteen years ago. I don't think he makes it a habit."

"And the other?" Samantha asked.

"Sexually," I said, "he knows what a woman wants, what she is feeling, what she is needing, and can give it to her until she screams for him to stop."

"Oh," Patty said.

Both women sat there silently, clearly lost in their own thoughts and imaginations.

At that moment I sure wanted Screamer's superpower, and would have traded two or three of my own to get it.

••◆ *8* ◆••

LOOKING FOR A GOD
IN ALL THE RIGHT PLACES

FOR A NUMBER OF YEARS, the World Series of Poker has been held mostly in the Horseshoe's old bingo hall on the second floor, with the cashier just inside the main door, and the tournament sign-up outside to the right in the hallway.

The World Series itself is a series of daily tournaments, with different levels of entry fees, called buy-ins, for each. I had hoped, when I arrived in town, to play in the fifteen hundred dollar buy-in, no-limit hold-em tournament that started tomorrow at noon. But now that I was helping Samantha, I would have to wait for another, later tournament.

The structure of a World Series tournament was fairly simple. You got as many tournament chips as the buy-in, then you played until only one person had all the chips. As you might imagine, that takes time, so for years the first day of every event ended when the final table, meaning the last nine players, was reached, and they started again the next day and finished off. For the last few years, they decided to just play to midnight, and everyone still left with chips came back the next day. Either way, it made for long tournaments, with the big tournament at the end of the five weeks costing ten thousand to buy-in, and lasting five days.

So, when I walked into the tournament room on the second floor of the Horseshoe, I could tell at once that there were still six tables in today's pot limit two thousand dollar buy-in hold-em tournament back in the far left corner of the room. Fifty or so players sweating to stay alive and make the top twenty to thirty positions that paid out money.

I glanced over at the electronic tournament board. Over three hundred players had started the tournament at noon and there was a first-place prize of almost two hundred thousand. There was nothing like the World Series of Poker for nice paydays. And one of those fifty players was going to pull it in.

All cash.

If I got a chance, I'd go back there later and watch a few hands.

Across the front of the room were live games with different betting limits. There were maybe forty tables of poker going at once, with a lot of people standing around talking and watching games. And across the back left of the room were satellite tournaments, where players played against each other to earn their buy-in into a bigger tournament. At the moment, there were a number of one-table events going on, with the winner on each table taking a full fifteen hundred in buy-in chips.

I liked playing satellites for warm-ups, and sometimes won my way into a big one. I planned this trip to play a bunch of what they called super-satellites until I earned my way into the ten thousand big event a month from now. Better than paying the full ten thousand out of my pocket, and more fun as well.

At first glance around the tournament room, I didn't see Stan. I didn't expect to, actually. Gambling Gods, when joining the ranks of the real players, tend to come in different shapes and sizes, and can disguise themselves very well.

"I understand you're looking for me?" a voice said from behind me as I stood near the cashier's area.

I turned around to face Stan, his long face smiling at me. He wasn't in any disguise, and was wearing his normal gray sweater and a baseball hat with no logo. His eyes were a gold and green and seemed to be able to stare right through me.

I hadn't told a person what I was going to do, yet Stan knew I was looking for him.

Scary. Damn scary.

I kept on my poker face and managed to say, "I am." I didn't ask him how he knew. "You have thirty seconds to talk privately?"

"Sure do," he said, nodding toward the small lobby outside at the top of the escalator.

The lobby was a place where deals were done, mostly between players who had no money, and people who did. The sponsors, as they were called, took a cut of a player's possible winnings in exchange for buying them into a tournament. Those arrangements were sometimes profitable for both sides, and often allowed a person who couldn't play top-level poker to ride along on the excitement with a person who could.

I led Stan over to an open spot against the wall. No one seemed to notice either of us, and I wondered if that was Stan blocking out people's attention, or just the fact that we looked like any two players trying to make a deal, which in essence, we were.

As soon as we got to a place where no one could hear us I asked him point blank, "You know what I'm working on?"

He nodded. "Trying to get a guy out of the hooks of some ghost slots." He laughed. "You always were a sucker for blind women and dogs."

"No contest there," I said, laughing with him, but not feeling that much at ease.

"And you're wondering if I have any advice on how to do what you and Screamer are trying to do?"

"Got me read in one," I said.

Stan nodded, as if thinking about how to play a hand. Then he looked directly at me. "Ghost slots are nasty things. And no one really knows how many of the things there are. They're always hungry, and they don't completely exist in the here and now. Some people say they can float through time and across distances, taking their human food with them. Once the human is drained of all energy and essence, they look for another snack."

That didn't sound good for Ben, that's for sure. "Any restrictions on the space or time they can move?"

Stan shrugged. "As far as I know, they can only travel to places where they once existed in real life, like those slots did here in the Horseshoe."

I nodded. I had figured as much, but it was good to hear him confirm that detail.

He went on. "They drive the God of Slots crazy, let me tell you. She thought she had them under control until this."

"I'll bet they get to her," I said, not feeling hopeful at all. If these things couldn't be handled by the Gambling Gods, what did a couple of superheroes like me and Screamer think we could do?

"You ever hear of anyone getting loose from them?"

"No," Stan said.

Then he stopped. I could sense that there was something he wasn't telling me. It felt odd to be reading the main God of Poker, but that was exactly what I was doing. I was putting a read on Stan.

"So what else is happening, Stan?"

Stan took a deep breath, and for a moment I thought he was going to just shake his head and say nothing. Then he glanced around.

Suddenly everyone froze. It felt as if we had moved between two moments in time.

Almost everyone around us had their mouth open, and the woman sitting at the sign-in table was in the process of adjusting her bra while looking down the hallway to her right.

Not only was everyone stopped like a statue, but Stan had shut off the sound as well, which in a casino can be very disconcerting. Casinos, the places I loved, were never completely quiet. Even in the slowest periods, slot machines made a humming noise, and often called out to customers to come play them, even though there were no customers around.

Every casino I knew had background music. Just the massive numbers of lights in casinos filled the places with a low noise. But now there wasn't a sound. Stan and I might have well been standing in the middle of the Mojave Desert without a wind.

"Nice trick," I said to Stan, nodding.

"Didn't want anyone hearing what I am about to tell you," Stan said.

"That good, huh?" I said, turning my attention from all the frozen people around me to Stan, suddenly very worried.

"Actually, that bad," Stan said. "The case you're working isn't the only ghost slot snatch. There have been around fifty, maybe a lot more, in the last six or seven days, and today someone got a reporter from the *Sun* to go stand in a certain spot in the Mirage and watch some slots take a woman."

"Someone is doing this on purpose?" I asked, just about as stunned and surprised as I had been in years.

"Looks that way," Stan said.

I made the next jump, to the only logical reason why anyone would be doing this purposely. "They're trying to kill every casino on the planet."

Stan nodded.

We both stood there in silence, the poker players and sponsors frozen around us like statues. The ideas that casinos were actually threatened just flat scared me beyond any monster, any killer I had ever faced. Casinos were my home, my place of power, the only reason I got up in the mornings.

Whoever was doing this was threatening me directly.

I turned to Stan. "The management has no leads on this?"

Management was what superheroes called the top gods.

"Everyone's working on it," Stan said. "I've been in two hundred casinos in the last few hours myself, looking for any clue, anything that might be a lead."

I nodded. If all the casino gods and management gods were on the case, I had no idea how Screamer and I could help. We were just a couple of lowly superheroes. And that thought came right out of my mouth next.

"So what good can I do in all this?"

Stan stared at me, and when the God of Poker stares at you, you know you've been studied, read, and put away. Never, in all my memory have I been looked at with that kind of intensity, that kind of focus, even by the best poker players in the world.

"Actually," Stan said after what seemed like the longest second I have ever survived, "you might be one of our best hopes. Burt told me this morning you were coming, would be working on this, and that I should help you where I can."

"Now I am really worried," I said.

"The managers of publicity and security have put a team together as well, a reporter and a cop. You might run into them, so help them if you can as well. All of us are after the same thing."

"Stopping these things," I said.

"Exactly," Stan said. "And soon."

I took a deep breath, glanced around at all the frozen statues of people filling the lobby at the top of the escalator, then turned back to face Stan.

"You said these ghost slots can move around when hunting, appearing and disappearing like the one I saw on that tape. Right?"

"That's what we always thought."

"So how can someone control something that can move like that?"

"You tell us that," Stan said, "and we'll know who's doing this."

I didn't really want to ask the next question, but I did. "Can it be another branch of gods, you know, the death and dying ones on some sort of strange crusade."

Stan shook his head. "No. I was there when Laverne checked with them."

Calling Lady Luck, the woman in charge of it all, by her first name, shook me. I would never have the courage to do that. Not ever. I wanted to keep playing and winning, and even though poker was a skill game, there was still that element of luck involved, and having the top of the top Herself mad at you would be a very, very bad thing.

"So we're dealing with someone who somehow has figured out a way to control ghost slots and wants casinos shut down. Some sort of anti-gambling nut-case."

"That's one of the main ways we're following as well. But my suggestion is that you track the slots to where they live here and now.

Their base, their nest, their haunt, whatever you want to call it. They have to go somewhere and you never know what you might find. And don't be afraid to use your Unstuck-In-Time power to follow them if you have to."

I nodded again, not completely understanding what he meant. I didn't know I had an Unstuck-In-Time superpower, and I wasn't sure what it might be, actually. But that was no surprise. Even after twenty years I was still discovering some of my powers.

"You mean I can do this?" I asked, motioning all the people around me. "How?"

"You can," he said. "When you need it, you'll know how."

"Well, thanks, I guess," I said. "You want me to report in to you."

"No need. I'll be following your progress and helping where I can," he said.

"Thanks, Stan," I said

"No problem," he said, smiling at me. "This is something special where we all need to help each other. I'll still owe you for passing up old Betty for me. Man, you got some will power. I hear she's about as good in the sack as they come."

With a laugh and a shake of his head, he turned away and headed back for the big room as everyone around us started moving again, and the noise pounded in like a dam breaking. I had no doubt that if I followed him in there I wouldn't be able to spot him again. Gambling Gods could disappear like that.

I headed for the elevator, doing my best to not think about what might have been that Christmas Eve with Betty, and that wonderful skin and perfect body of hers. I had a blind woman's husband to rescue, the entire casino industry to save, and maybe a new superpower to use. It just wasn't the right moment for me to be thinking about wild sex.

By the time I had reached my room, I had replaced Betty's face in my mind with Patty's wonderful smile, brown hair, raspberry smell, and perfect mole.

But even her wonderful face and the memory of her smell couldn't keep the images of empty casinos, boarded up and shut down forever, from filling my thoughts.

I'd have to hang up my Poker Boy jacket and hat and go to playing poker in back rooms, bars, and Elk clubs to make a living. It wouldn't be a bad life, but it wouldn't be a great one either.

I spent most of the rest of the night on my bed, fully dressed, with my superhero uniform still on, soaking up the energy and thinking.

⋅•♦ 9 ♦•⋅

TOO DAMN EARLY

SCREAMER CALLED what seemed like five minutes after I had finally managed to doze off.

Somehow, I got the phone on the second, maybe third ring, and got it to the side of my face without hurting myself. Then, before I mumbled the word "Hello," he started talking.

"No luck so far, Poker Boy. But I think I got a lead. It's out in one of the old joints on the highway toward the dam. You want me to follow it?"

"Yeah," I said, fighting to get my mind focused on what he was saying and not the fading dream of spending a night with a beautiful gambling god.

"Also, this is a lot bigger than we thought," Screamer said.

That snapped me awake, remembering what Stan had talked to me about, what had kept me laying awake thinking all night.

"What do you know?"

"Looks like most of the police and the newspaper are onto this, and a lot of people have been taken, not just Ben. So far, everyone's keeping a lid on things, but I doubt, and so do others, that lid's going to hold much longer."

My stomach twisted. The last thing we needed at this point was a panic, a mass exodus away from casinos and Las Vegas.

"Heard you talked to Stan last night," Screamer said. "Did he give us any help?"

"Some," I said, surprised that Screamer knew I had met with a gambling god. Maybe Screamer had done the same thing. "Stan told me how big this problem really is, gave me a couple of warnings and a suggestion or two."

"Good," he said. "I'll chase down what leads I can, then catch up with you and Patty at the diner. How does around noon sound?"

"Perfect," I said. "Thanks, Screamer."

"No problem," he said. "You just be careful. From everything I hear these ghost slots are not something to be fooled with lightly. And I doubt that if there are people behind this mess, they are either."

"Stan said the same thing. You watch your back as well."

"Doing just that," Screamer said. "No worries, we'll tackle them together."

With that he hung up, leaving me holding the phone and very much awake. And very glad he was helping me.

The clock on the nightstand said two minutes after six in the morning. Way too early for a poker player to get up.

Poker players are, by the nature of the game, night people. I have seen six in the morning more times than I want to think about, but always from the night side, almost never from the morning side. I don't care what anyone says, getting out of bed before the sun comes up is just not natural.

Still, with Screamer's words echoing in my mind, I bid a final goodbye to the last dream-thoughts of a gambling goddess, climbed out of bed and did all the things a person, or superhero, does to get ready for a day.

By seven in the morning, the sun was up, and I was drinking coffee and reading the morning newspaper in the diner across Front Street from the Horseshoe.

I silently thanked all the gambling gods that Madge wasn't there.

The paper had three reports of people going missing, but they were scattered and buried. Only one report mentioned the fact that the person had vanished from a casino. All three were tourists and the newspaper said the police were working at their cases. The big story was staying buried.

So far so good.

At a few minutes after eight, Samantha, her dog, Sue, and Patty joined me.

Patty somehow managed to be stunning, even early in the morning. She wore no make-up, faded jeans, and a tucked-in white blouse that gave just enough hint of the white lace-trimmed bra underneath to be alluring. Her hair seemed to shine in the diner light, and she had pulled it back exposing my favorite mole for the entire world to see.

Samantha, on the other hand, looked like she hadn't slept all night, had barely managed to get dressed this morning, and was in desperate need of coffee. Not even her black glasses could hide the rings under her eyes.

"Good morning, ladies," I said, tossing my paper aside and standing to let them join me in the booth.

Patty gave me a beaming smile and a "Good morning to you as well."

Then she helped Samantha into the booth and stepped back as Sue curled up at her master's feet.

"How was your night?" Patty asked as she slid into the booth and against the wall on my side. "You or Toledo get any leads?"

"Screamer's following one now," I said, doing my best to ignore her wonderful raspberry smell and the closeness of her arm against mine in the booth. "He's going to meet us back here at noon."

"Good," Patty said.

I kept talking because it was the only way I knew to not just stare at her.

"I talked to a friend of mine last night up in the tournament room, called in a marker, and got a little help as well."

Patty turned sideways, moving her arm away from mine so she could look at me with a steady gaze. "Anyone I know?"

"Not unless you know some of the gambling gods," I said, smiling at her, pretending to be joking. I often figured that the best way to tell someone something they wouldn't believe, and get them to change the subject, was to flat tell them the truth.

"Oh, yeah, right," Samantha said from the other side of the booth, shaking her head in clear disgust.

Patty, on the other hand, kept staring at me, then just nodded slightly.

I was starting to gain a lot of respect for Patty. Clearly my current sidekick knew a lot more about the behind-the-scenes working of Las Vegas and the gambling world than I was giving her credit for.

Plus, she was beautiful, smelled wonderful, and had hair a person could get lost in while searching closely for a mole.

"I'm going to the police again right after breakfast," Samantha said, clearly upset, as she had every right to be. "I'm going to make them start looking for Ben if I have to stand there and just scream."

"Good idea," I said, turning my attention from the allure of my sidekick to the task at hand. "You never know when we might need their help."

I didn't tell her that I had no doubt the police were already working on finding Ben. And all of the others taken by the slots before him.

Samantha seemed a little surprised that I had agreed with her that quickly. Clearly, she still thought we were trying to run some scam on her, and had discounted the images of her husband Screamer had put into her mind last night. I didn't blame her. Believing that a person could be taken by ghost slot machines wasn't easy, even for someone like me who was used to the strange happenings.

Many, many of the people I help don't believe I can help them at first. It's an occupational hazard of being a superhero. In fact, I bet if there was ever a convention of superheroes, and we had panels and meetings about the problems we all faced, this would be one of the main topics of discussion. After all the years, I had gotten used to it, and having a person like Samantha not believe in the real problem didn't even surprise me.

"I agree," Patty said, nodding to me, then turning to talk directly to Samantha. "I'll be glad to drive you down to the main station after breakfast. I have a detective friend there that will waive the forty-eight hour waiting period for me if I ask real nice."

I'd waive anything if she asked nice, but I didn't say that out loud.

"Thank you," Samantha said, some of the anger draining from her posture. "That would be really helpful."

"Help is why we're here," I said. "Besides, they frown on people standing in the lobby of the police station screaming. It gives Las Vegas a bad image."

Patty gave me a beaming smile that reached her eyes, and Samantha actually laughed as the waitress came up to take our order.

The morning waitress wasn't a lot better than Madge in looks, but clearly younger by about twenty years, and lighter by forty pounds. Her name was Fran, her hair was bleached blonde, and her make-up heavy in the purple eye-liner department. The coffee pot in her right hand seemed to be glued there as she listened to our orders, asked the right toast and hash-brown questions, and then went off with a "Got it."

She hadn't written anything down, which seemed almost magical to me. How could she remember all that, plus have a conversation with the booth next to ours while refilling their coffee cups? Of course, what I do at a poker table looks like magic to some people, so I guess it's just where a person's focus is. And where they make their living.

Who knows, maybe Fran was a superhero in the waitressing world. Maybe she went around saving truck drivers with bad body odor with the help of the waitressing gods. I know for a fact there are such things as evil bacon, and Mexican food with a bite. So why couldn't there be superhero waitresses who rush in to save the day like we're trying to do with Ben?

"So what's the plan?" Patty asked after Fran left.

"Well," I said, "after we help Samantha get Ben officially reported as missing with the police, you and I could do some tracking. My source last night tells me the best thing to do is try to track the machines to where they live, which I assume meant where the old machines are stored."

"You think they're stored and haven't been destroyed?" Patty asked.

"I would bet just about anything on it," I said. "My source also told me they can only move around in the time frame which they existed, which means since Ben was taken yesterday, those things still exist somewhere."

"We just have to find them," Patty said, nodding. "Which means we have to figure out where the old Valley Slots graveyard is."

"Wouldn't it be owned by Standard Slots now?" I asked. "Since they bought out Valley a long time ago?"

"More than likely," Patty said. "I called my dad last night and he gave me a name to contact at Standard Slots. But he seems to think that there is still a Valley Slots graveyard somewhere."

"Graveyard?" Samantha asked, clearly not liking the sound of the term.

"It's what they call the monster warehouses in which they store the old slot machines," I said.

"Why don't they just haul them to the dump?" Samantha asked.

I shrugged. "Honestly, I'm not one hundred percent certain, but from what I've heard over the years, it has to do with their value. Some are junked, others have parts switched out to working machines, but by-and-large, they just store the things."

"I heard it was taxes," Patty said. "And corporate valuation. A corporation just can't go throwing away assets, even though the assets have no real use any more. Plus, I think there are regs that make junking a slot machine more expensive than just renting a giant warehouse and storing them in mass."

Samantha nodded, then asked, "So how many machines are in these storage places?"

"I doubt anyone knows," I said. "I've seen basements full of the things, warehouses stacked with them, and hallways in the backs of hotels lined with the things."

"Oh," Samantha said. "And you think you're going to find four of them from more than a decade ago?"

Patty and I sat there looking at each other, not answering her. Samantha had a point. Las Vegas was a haystack made up of hundreds and hundreds of thousands of slot machines. And we weren't even looking for a needle. We were looking for a piece of hay.

A very old piece of hay.

··◆*10*◆··

A NAP AND A SEARCH

I TOOK A NAP right after breakfast. Yes, superheroes take naps. I know that blows the image built with decades of comic books and movies, but it is true. It's just tough for those comic book artists to draw naps, and besides, when naps are done right, they're really boring.

My nap was done perfectly.

After breakfast, Patty took Samantha down to the police station to file the missing person's report. She was going to call me in my room when she got back.

I had intended on making a few phone calls to find out what had happened to Valley Slot's slot graveyards, but it only took one call to a friend of mine at city hall to get the address of what he thought was the only Valley Slots graveyard left, owned, of course, by Standard Slots.

I sort of remember sitting there on the bed after hanging up the phone. The soft bedspread had looked so inviting.

What would it hurt to just stretch out and think for a few minutes? I told myself that.

Just think.

Patty's call woke me an hour later. It was six minutes before ten in the morning.

"Any luck?" Patty asked without saying hello.

The sound of her voice had me instantly awake. "Yeah, got us an address. I'll be right down."

"Meet you in front of the main desk. I'm double-parked so don't take long."

She hung up.

I sat there for a moment wondering if I had just dreamt that call, finally convincing myself I hadn't.

I tossed a handful of water on my face, combed my hair enough so that it wouldn't look slept on, put on my hat and Poker Boy leather coat, and headed out the door.

By the time I hit the lobby, I was feeling much, much better, and ready for a day of work.

"Good nap?" Patty asked, smiling at me.

I managed to not show I was surprised at the question. "Naps are always good."

Patty laughed. "You poker players are all alike."

"A society of nappers, huh?"

"Pro nappers," she said, still laughing as she led the way out of the casino and into the warm morning air.

I could tell the day was going to be hot again. Considering it was still April, I would wager the high desert was going to be in for a really hot year.

Patty had a new model Honda, which looked a lot like most other mid-sized cars being made. It was the first halfway-plain thing I had seen about her. But even though it was a dull design, the inside of the car was clean, the air conditioning kept me comfortable, and the car had acceleration enough to get through traffic just fine.

Patty drove like a professional, smooth and direct, changing lanes when she needed to, and driving ahead, watching for problems. And she didn't tailgate. So far, even with a dull, regular car, there was nothing about this woman I didn't like.

When I gave Patty the address I had gotten from my friend in city hall, she started out what was called the Old Boulder Highway without hesitation. They've built a freeway along the same route, but Patty stayed on the old highway, going past the dozens of strip malls, old motels, and small casinos that lined every mile of the old highway.

What people think of as Las Vegas was actually made up of four medium-small cities. There was Las Vegas, North Las Vegas, Henderson, and Boulder City. There were actually a number of other smaller towns as well, but they had been pretty much swallowed by the growth of the other four.

I let Patty focus on her driving while I worked on how we were going to get into the warehouse. We sure couldn't just tell whoever was guarding the place that we were looking for the home of a ghost slot machine. Never work.

By the time Patty turned off the old highway onto a side road just south of Whitney, which is sometimes called East Las Vegas, I had us a cover story.

She pulled the car into the tumbleweed-covered parking lot of a giant warehouse and put it in park, letting the air-conditioning run on low. She looked at the huge metal building and then turned to me with a smile. "Now what?"

I could see the faded address numbers on the side of the building. It was clear that unless there was a security guard roaming the place, we weren't going to need a cover story. From the looks of this building, I doubted anyone had been around it for years. The desert sun had taken the metal to a dull gray, and the winds and sand had removed any sign that the place might have been painted at one time in the past.

"We go in, I guess," I said, shrugging. "And in case anyone stops us, we're thinking about working on a book about old slot machines, and trying to get an idea what some of them looked like."

"Good cover story," she said, nodding. "But I doubt we're going to need it here. More than likely, we're going to have to go to the Standard Slots main office and get someone to bring us back and let us in."

"Yeah," I said, shoving the door open, "but we should take a look around first."

I was hoping we wouldn't have to waste time going to the main office, and with what Stan had told me, I really didn't want anyone from Standard Slots to know we were even looking around, just in case they were involved with the kidnappings. It never hurt to be careful.

The highway noise from a few blocks over cut through the warm air as we started toward what looked to be a main door. The warehouse had four large, drive-in bay doors and a regular-sized door beside the bay door on the left.

Since I was a good block from the closest casino, I wasn't sure if my superpowers would work. Sometimes, I had what I called hold-over powers if I had spent a lot of time in a casino right before I needed the power. Spending the night in the Horseshoe might be enough, and having a small casino a block away would be a little help. At least I hoped it would, because I was going to try using a power I very seldom got to use. I called it my Open-Says-Me Power.

It worked like a charm the few times I had had to use it on locked casino doors. I had no idea if it would work on this warehouse door.

"Looks closed up tight," Patty said. "I'll bet no one has even checked on this place in six months."

"True," I said, shrugging. "But maybe we'll get lucky."

I took hold of the door knob and then, focusing my power like I was studying a guy trying to bluff me off a pair of queens, I turned the knob and heard the dead-bolt slide back. I smiled at Patty and opened the door.

The door made a scraping sound on the sidewalk as it opened, and let out cool, musty-smelling air from the dark inside.

"Looks like we got lucky," Patty said. She was shaking her head and half frowning at me. But I could see amusement in her eyes as well, and maybe a little fondness. Or maybe I just hoped to see the fondness.

"Hello!" I shouted into the warehouse as I stepped into the darkness.

The sound of my shout echoed back at me.

"No one home," Patty said, moving in to stand beside me, leaving the door open behind us. "Now that's a surprise."

"The trick is going to be finding the lights," I said.

I went left along the wall, Patty moved right. A moment later I heard a few loud clicks from Patty's direction and the warehouse flooded with light.

"Oh, my," Patty said, moving over to stand by me as I stared at what stretched out in front of us.

The place looked a lot bigger inside than it did outside, with fourteen aisles big enough to drive a forklift through. And on each side of every aisle, sometimes stacked in crates, were slot machines.

"There have to be thousands in here," Patty said.

"Easily," I said. Actually, I figured there were closer to ten thousand different slot machines facing us.

I focused my powers again, concentrating, trying to get any feeling, any of my powers to help me find the slot machines we were looking for.

Suddenly, in front of me, I could see a faint orange glow that sort of led off to the far wall and down that aisle. Superpowers still working fine it seemed. Now I'd have to come up with a name for this power.

"This way," I said, heading with the glow.

We went along the front of the big closed bay doors and then along the wall, moving past old slot machines covered in dust, some protected by either plastic wraps or tarps. All their lights were dark, their colors faded, covered in dust, or completely gone. Many had holes in their fronts from being cannibalized, many had broken arms and broken displays.

"This is damned creepy," Patty said.

"That it is," I said. "I see why they call it a graveyard."

"No kidding," Patty said.

Even with the bright overhead lights on, the canyons of old slot machines seemed to radiate old age. Though the old slots had at one time been colorful, their colors didn't seem to have made it here. Everything around us was in shades of gray.

I had the feeling as we moved along that we were walking deeper and deeper into the past. And not just because of the age of the machines around us.

It was something else.

Something very real that my Danger-Ahead Superpower was telling me wasn't good.

The orange glow stopped at a covered bank of slot machines. Under the faded black tarp loomed a shape that looked like the Saturn Slots we had seen in the security footage.

I stopped a few steps away and motioned that Patty should do the same. "Stay here."

"You think those are the ones?" Patty asked. "How would you know?"

"Just a hunch."

I moved the last few steps forward, reached up and grabbed the tarp covering the slots. Then with all my strength, I yanked.

The tarp came easily, spreading into a pile in the middle of the aisle, pushing rolling clouds of dust into the air.

I had stepped back beside Patty as I pulled, and then when the slots were exposed, we both stepped back another two steps.

What faced us couldn't be there, yet it was.

Four Saturn Slots, with four wooden chairs attached, the bright image of the planet and its rings dominating everything. We had found what we were looking for all right.

But there was a problem.

It was turned on.

Every light on the machines was working, the chrome and brass polished and shining, as if it were sitting on a casino floor just waiting for a customer.

I could feel the attraction to sit down, to just play one nickel.

And I had never once put one coin into a slot machine.

Never.

Ever.

I wasn't a gambler. I was a poker player.

Around us, the gray of the dust-filled warehouse took on colors reflecting from the machine. Every warning alarm I had in my body went off. It was as if by uncovering the thing, we were spreading its power.

"Why would someone leave it plugged in?" Patty asked, her voice almost a whisper.

"I'm fairly certain it's not plugged into anything that pretends to be electricity," I said. "It's getting its power from something else, somewhere else."

I could feel them tugging us toward them, as if they were saying *"What would it hurt to sit down and just play a nickel?"*

I took Patty's arm and pulled her a few staggering steps backward as the lights from the machine got brighter. Clearly, the machines were affecting her as much as they were trying to get to me.

Suddenly, the warehouse was filled with a man's shout, echoing through the cavernous space.

"Police! Who's in here?"

"Far aisle on the right side of the door as you come in!" I shouted. "Hurry!"

I figured the police were here for the same reason we were, and I wanted them to see these machines before they vanished, as I had a hunch they were about to do.

I pulled Patty a few more steps backward down the aisle as the machine started to pulse, its colors gaining and then losing intensity.

Behind us, I could hear the running footsteps of the police.

In front of us, the ghost slots were glowing brighter than any slot I had ever seen, filling all the old slots around them with color and light.

Then, as if I was watching a movie, I saw flashes of images flicker around the slots, different people, different casino backgrounds, clearly even different time periods.

The images came faster and faster as the pulses of light from the slot machine got brighter and brighter.

The image of Ben flashed past, the same as we had seen in the Horseshoe's security cameras.

Then the image of a middle-aged woman, then a young man and his girlfriend together, then more and more, maybe dozens of people, until suddenly the pulsing light stopped.

The Saturn Slots were gone, an empty space remaining in the rows of old slot machines.

The warehouse went back to a dirty gray, washed out by the overhead white lights.

Patty leaned against me. "Oh, my," she said softly.

I moved my arm around her waist. Having her that close to me felt right, felt nice. I just wished it were for a different reason.

"Holy shit," a woman said behind us, her voice a hoarse whisper.

I glanced around at a man and woman standing a dozen steps behind us, still staring at where the Saturn Slots had been a moment before.

The man, a Detective I knew named Johnny State, had his gun out, but it was hanging in his hand, looking very useless.

I turned back to look at the empty space where the Saturn Slots had been a moment before.

It was still empty.

The slots were out hunting.

But what happened to the people they took?

Who was controlling such an amazing monster?

And even a better question yet: What were we going to do to stop it?

··◆ 11 ◆··

THE RETURN FROM HELL

JOHNNY AND I had just finished putting the tarp back in place when the energy of the big warehouse started to change again.

I had had a lot of natural powers before becoming Poker Boy, and one of them was the ability to sense when the energy in something was changing. Usually, I used that sense in a poker game, or when someone was starting to get angry. Now I could feel it in the air around us.

I took Johnny by the arm and pulled him away from where we had been staring at the tarp being held up by empty space, moving us and Patty and the woman, Geneva, even farther away down the aisle.

Suddenly bright colors seemed to flash through the gaps in the tarp and the machines were back. I could feel the pull of them, the desire to have someone come to them and sit down.

"Those things are hungry," Patty said softly as the four of us backed even farther away.

"Let's go back to the door," I said, touching Johnny's arm to get him to move.

As I touched his skin, I got a sense of Geneva with him as well. For a second it was as if there were three of us in the same head.

I let go of Johnny's arm and glanced at him as we headed away from the machines.

"Weird, huh?" he said, shrugging.

Clearly he knew I had joined them for a moment.

Geneva had her hand on Johnny's arm. I knew at once it was touch that linked the two of them, and for some reason my touch had linked me with them for a second as well.

"How long?" I asked.

"Since we met yesterday," Johnny said.

"Doesn't work without touch?" I asked.

"Not yet," Johnny said.

We had turned the corner out of the aisle of old slots with the dangerous machines and the pull from them was almost gone.

"What are you two talking about?" Patty asked. "Include the rest of us if you would, please."

I knew Geneva had understood and been part of Johnny's side of the conversation, since the two of them were linked. But I doubted they wanted Patty to know, and if they did, they would tell her.

"Oh, sorry," I said. "Just trying to figure out who could control those monsters back there."

Geneva laughed. "It's all right if she knows, since you do, and we are all working together on this."

All four of us stopped near the front door. It was standing open and the bright light from outside was pouring in, overwhelming the warehouse lights. The inside of the warehouse seemed almost alien compared to the life, the bright light, and the distant traffic outside. I could also feel the warm air flooding in.

Geneva touched Johnny's arm as she faced Patty. "For some reason, the how or why of which we don't understand, Detective State and I have a link telepathically when we touch. We discovered this wonderful gift yesterday when we met."

Johnny was nodding.

Patty stared at Geneva for a moment, then turned to me. "And you knew this how?"

"Got a flash of it when I touched Johnny when steering us away from back there."

Patty shook her head at me. "You are sure full of surprises."

"He is at that," Johnny said, laughing. Then, without giving Patty a chance to ask any questions about what Geneva had told her, he went on. "So what next?"

I shrugged. "We found the machines and now we have more questions than we did before. I'm struggling with someone having the ability to control those things back there, if they are what they appear."

"And if they aren't, who's doing the illusions?" Patty said.

"And why?" Johnny said. "Most of the police department is on this case, tracking anti-gambling groups, religious nut-cases, and anything else they can think of. By now I'm pretty sure that even the Feds are involved, maybe the anti-terrorist bunch as well."

That all made sense to me. You just can't have fifty people or more vanish in a week from a city and not stir up everything. It was amazing that it wasn't all over the television and papers.

"For the moment, we're the only one's following these slots, right?"

Johnny nodded. "Geneva was sent to me because someone sent a note to the *Sun* to have a reporter stand at the Mirage to watch something."

"So you saw these things take someone?"

"I did," Geneva said. "The Saturn Slots sort of faded in right over a bank of slots in the Mirage, a middle-aged woman sat down, put in a nickel, and the slots and the woman vanished."

"Same thing that happened to Ben at the Horseshoe," Patty said. "We watched it on a security tape that no longer exists."

Geneva laughed. "We discovered last night that the Mirage's tape of the area shows nothing, including me standing there."

"No surprise," I said. "They are not going to use their own security tapes to condemn their own business."

"So someone's directing these things," Johnny said. "We need to figure out how, or who, or from where?"

My little voice was going off like an alarm bell. This happened all the time when I was about to make a call with a hand in a poker game that was statistically right, yet felt wrong. Once I learned to lay down the hands that my little voice told me to lay down, I started earning a lot more money.

"Back up half a step," I said. I turned to Geneva. "You said you got a note to go to a place and stand and see what happens. Right?"

Geneva nodded.

"Nothing more? Nothing about kidnapping, or ghost slots or anything?"

"That's right," she said.

"So we have a second option," I said. "Someone might not be controlling those things. They may only be predicting them."

I looked at the three puzzled faces staring at me and managed to not laugh. "Machines are machines," I said. "They are governed by programming and statistical payouts. Why wouldn't a ghost slot be working under the same basic rules? And if that's the case, it might be logical the slots are following a pattern that someone could predict."

"Possible," Johnny said. "But I'm still leaning toward someone in direct control somewhere. This entire mess has the potential of bringing down casinos all over the world. The payoff's too big to not have someone in control of it."

Geneva was clearly agreeing with Johnny, and since she was touching his arm, I knew that what Johnny had said went for both of them. Which was fine. We had a fork in the road of possibilities here. They would chase down one, Patty and I and Screamer would chase the other one. For all I knew, it was a combination of both.

"So how long until the lid blows off this thing?" I asked Geneva.

"Not long," she said. "A day, maybe two at most. Sooner if someone besides us puts the slot machine angle firmly on the disappearances."

"Okay," I said. "Johnny, can you keep a lid on this warehouse, not even let the owners in here?"

"I can," he said. "I'll get a patrol car out here to sit and keep everyone but the four of us out." He patted his back pocket. "We have a search warrant. I'll just say we're not done searching yet."

"Make sure the cops you put on this don't come inside," I said. "Last thing we need is a cop getting taken by those things."

"Agreed," Johnny said.

I kept on talking, sort of taking control of the investigation without really giving anyone else the chance to. "Patty and I have a lunch meeting with Screamer. We'll follow up on the idea that someone might have the ability to predict a ghost slot and try to figure out who sent you that note."

"We've both got to report back in at work," Geneva said, "see if anything else has broke." She smiled. "Don't worry, not one word that we've found these things yet."

Johnny nodded his agreement.

"Thanks," I said.

I had no doubt that if the entire mess broke open, she would have to tell her boss, and write the story. And if she was as linked as I thought she was with Johnny, she would leave Patty and me out of it. That had been my deal with Johnny back when I helped him solve that murder case. He'd taken all the credit, I'd helped a guy named Brian get out of jail, and even managed to rescue a Great Dane in the process from a flash flood up in the mountains.

That had turned out to be a good trip to Vegas. Man and dog both safe and free, a new police detective as a friend, and over twenty thousand in poker winnings at the same time. A superhero can't ask for many better trips than that one had been.

"So how about we meet back here at six?" Johnny said. "Compare notes, see if we can figure out a way to study that thing back there."

"Six," I said. "I'll call you if we come up with anything quicker."

"Great," Johnny said.

With that, Patty and I headed out into the bright mid-day sun.

Johnny and Geneva shut the warehouse door behind us and got into Johnny's unmarked police car. I saw Johnny immediately pick up the mike and call for a car to come watch the warehouse.

Patty and I were back on the Boulder Highway heading into town before the air conditioning actually started to work and fight back the oven-like interior of her car. For the second day I wondered about taking off my superhero costume and then decided against it. Besides, Patty's car would eventually cool down.

We rode in silence for a few stoplights. I was trying to wrap my mind around the fact that those machines left the warehouse, yet they never really did, since their shape could still hold up a tarp. I had seen a lot of very strange things in my days as a superhero, but nothing like that. I felt I almost needed a scientist to explain what was happening.

Or a magician if the entire thing was an illusion. I didn't think it was, but yet I couldn't exclude the chance completely.

Maybe Stan might know how that worked, or know who to ask. I'd have to find him after lunch. Besides, it might not hurt for me to check in with Stan and see if the gods of gambling were having any more luck than the police were.

"Poker Boy, huh?" Patty said as we sat waiting for the third stoplight. "Where'd that name come from?"

I glanced sideways at her. She was half-smiling, staring at the intersection, knowing that she had me pinned.

"It's just what people have called me for years," I said. "I've been thinking of changing that to Poker Man because of the gray in my hair, but so far I haven't bothered."

Patty actually had the decency to laugh and not ask anything more.

·•◆ *12* ◆•·

A QUICK LUNCH

BY THE TIME PATTY AND I had gotten Samantha and her dog, Sue, out of her room at the Horseshoe Hotel, and the four of us had made it to the little café, it was ten before noon. Madge, the waitress, was there again, along with the woman from the breakfast shift. I managed to keep focused on Patty and her wonderful raspberry smell and avoided looking at Madge when she walked away from our table popping her gum.

Screamer joined us before we even had our drinks, sliding in beside me on one side of the booth and smiling at the two women.

"Hello again, Samantha," he said. "Police have any luck?"

"Nothing," Samantha said.

From the way she had been walking and the sound of her voice, I could tell she was tired and very down. In her situation, with a loving

85

husband suddenly gone for no reason, I didn't blame her. Actually, I thought she was holding up very well, considering the circumstances.

"Well," I said, "now that all of us are here, let me tell you what Patty and I found out this morning. First off, we met with Detective Johnny State and reporter Geneva Gurwell from the *Sun*."

Screamer whistled softly. "You're playing with fire with Geneva. She's known as a tough reporter, maybe the best the *Sun* has."

"We know," Patty said. "And Detective State is no slouch either. The good thing for you to know, Samantha, is that just about the entire police department is working on this."

"And more than likely the FBI as well," I said.

"On Ben's disappearance?" Samantha asked, turning her head toward Patty.

"His, and a lot of other disappearances over the past week," Patty said, putting her hand gently on Samantha's. "It seems that whatever happened to Ben has happened more than fifty times this past week."

"Started nine days ago," Screamer said. "Sixty-seven people officially missing, another dozen maybes, there could be even more. And that's all I was able to get the entire morning."

I glanced at Screamer. Clearly his sources had gotten us the same basic information Patty and I got from Stan and Johnny and Geneva.

"Over seventy people?" Samantha asked, her voice soft.

"Looks that way," I said. "That's why so many people are working on this, which is a good thing."

Samantha nodded. "I guess so."

The silence filled the booth. I wasn't letting myself believe that those seventy people might be dead. Even though I had seen Ben disappear on that tape, I had to believe he was still alive somewhere. Otherwise, this was going to be one of the biggest mass-murders in modern times. But until I learned otherwise, I was going to go on the belief that we were rescuing people, not trying to stop a killer.

"We also found the Saturn Slots," Patty said. "We watched them vanish and return right up close."

"You're kidding?" Screamer said. "You saw the ghost slots where they lived?"

"That we did," I said.

"Oh, man," Screamer said, "you two have more guts than brains. Those things are monsters."

"That they are," a man's voice said from beside me at the end of the table.

All four of us turned like our heads were on the same string.

Stan was pulling up a chair to sit, moving carefully to avoid Sue on the floor.

I didn't know what to think. In all my life I had never heard of a gambling god joining someone for lunch. I supposed they had to eat, but having a god at lunch just seemed downright strange.

Besides that, the service was going to be damned slow, since everyone in the restaurant and outside the restaurant was frozen in place. Clearly Stan had moved our table into a place between moments in time. Luckily, Madge was on the other side of the café and had been coming toward us when Stan arrived.

After Stan got settled, he reached across in front of me. "Screamer, great to meet you. I've heard a lot about you."

Screamer shook his hand. "Stan, the pleasure's all mine."

"Patty," Stan said, turning to her, smiling. "It's been a while."

"Stan," Patty said, smiling back. "Nice seeing you again."

I stared at the woman I had met across the front desk at the Horseshoe like she was an alien. She clearly knew Stan better than I did, and from the smile she gave him, they had a history I wasn't sure I wanted to know about.

I am a poker player. I am supposed to be able to read people, get a clear idea of who they are, what they are going to do in any situation. Patty and Stan had just shown me my reading powers when it came to Patty were non-existent. I had met a couple of people over the years that could block my reads, but not many. Not many at all. And for some reason, I hadn't thought of Patty as one of those people. But she was. She could block my reads on her without me even knowing I was being blocked.

She was good.

Very good.

I glanced across the table at Samantha, who had a puzzled frown on her face.

"Samantha," I said, "the man who just joined us is named Stan. Stan, Samantha."

I figured there was no point in trying to tell her he was one of the gods of gambling. She had enough weird stuff to deal with as it was.

Samantha brought her hand up to shake Stan's hand and he took it.

"Very nice meeting you," he said. "Even though you aren't a gambler. But rest assured, this group can get your husband back if anyone can."

"Thank you," Samantha said. "I'm slowly starting to believe that. And I don't think I really want to know how you shut down every person and every noise around us, do I?"

"Nothing harmful, I assure you," Stan said, a smile on his face that Samantha couldn't see, but I was sure she knew was there.

She nodded and asked nothing more.

"So," Stan said, turning back to face me and Screamer. "You found the home of the ghost slots."

"Right where they were supposed to be," I said. "They sort of left and came back while we were there."

"*Sort of* is right," Patty said.

Stan looked at her, then back at me, as puzzled as I ever wanted to see a god be.

"The things were covered with a tarp when we found them," I said. "Patty and I pulled the tarp off just before they vanished. But then Geneva realized that if the things were coming and going, they couldn't have been under a tarp, so Detective State and I put the tarp back into place, showing that some invisible part of the slot machines stayed in the warehouse."

"Now that's damn weird," Screamer said.

"But you couldn't see anything that was there?" Stan asked.

"Nothing," I said. "But that heavy tarp was being held up by something in the shape of the Saturn Slots. And when the slots returned, the tarp didn't move one bit."

"And there was no person sitting in one of the chairs?" Screamer asked.

"Nothing the tarp showed in form or movement," Patty said.

"Magic trick," Samantha said. "Sounds like a magic trick Ben and I saw back before we were married at the Mirage. Those two men with white tigers did that sort of thing."

"It's a standard magic illusion," Stan said. "But there's nothing magic going on with these machines. That much I can tell you. We've checked that side out."

Screamer, Patty and I were all nodding. If a gambling god said it wasn't something, it wasn't. They had sources I didn't want to think about, and more than likely those sources had gone into the world of magic, talked to the gods that controlled magic and illusion, and got that cleared.

"So," Screamer said, "if it's not an illusion, what's powering those things?"

Stan looked at Screamer. "That's a good question. We haven't looked into that side of this yet. I will meet with Burt and Laverne as soon as we get done here to have them go after that side of things."

With the mention of Laverne's name, I wanted to almost bow my head. I could see Patty's eyes get big as well at the name. When Stan talked about Laverne, he talked about Lady Luck herself, the General Manager of all Gambling.

"Good," Screamer said, clearly as stunned as I felt at Stan's off-handed mention of Laverne.

"Stan," I said, "you mentioned there were other teams working on this."

"Sure," Stan said.

"Detective State and Geneva Gurwell are one team, right?"

"They are," Stan said. "They were given some powers to help them."

"Well," I said, "have you heard the information they have about someone pointing Geneva to a place where the slots would show up, before they showed up."

Now it was Stan's turn to stare at me, and again it felt as if I was being read by the best poker player on the planet.

"I *didn't* know that."

"Detective State and Geneva are working on the angle that someone can control the machines," Patty said. "We're going after the chance that someone can predict the things."

"Any suggestions on that?" I asked. "Who we should talk to, who might be able to predict or control ghost slots?"

"I can't imagine anyone controlling those things," Stan said. "Not even Maggie, who's in charge of slots, knows how or why those things work. They have been a thorn in the side of her department since slots were invented."

"So I want to know," Samantha said, "how machines can take my husband and all these other people? Where do the people go? Where's Ben right now?"

"We don't know that either I'm afraid," Stan said.

"If the machines are being controlled, they might be dropping the victims off in a third location," Patty said.

"But if they aren't controlled and someone is only predicting them, that's going to help us as well," I said.

"Talk to The Bookkeeper," Stan said. "He might have been the one who sent the note to the *Sun*."

I had never heard of anyone called The Bookkeeper, but clearly Patty and Screamer had from the looks of disgust on their faces.

"Where can we find this guy?" I asked.

"He's got a home out in West Las Vegas," Patty said, before Stan could answer. Her voice seemed suddenly angry and clearly disgusted. On this topic, I was having no problem at all reading her.

"Don't like the guy, huh?" I said, smiling at Patty.

"No one likes the guy," Patty said. "He's a pig."

"Amen to that," Screamer said.

"Well, at the moment, he's still our best lead," I said. Then I turned to Stan. "You're going to check on the power source question, right?"

"I am," Stan said. "I'll find you and let you know what we come up with."

"Thanks," I said.

I turned to Screamer. "Would you use your sources and find us the best old-slot technician you can find. It needs to be someone who can work on the slots as old as those Saturn Slots. And someone who can still move and get things done."

Screamer nodded. "Sure, but why?"

"If these things really are just out-of-control machines functioning on statistics and mechanics, we're going to need someone who knows what makes them tick."

"Gotcha," Screamer said. "And you and Patty get The Bookkeeper."

"Oh, yuch," Patty said.

"And what can I do to help?" Samantha asked.

I stared at Samantha for a moment. It wasn't often that someone I was trying to help asked to help in the process. In this case, I didn't blame her one bit. If I had been in her position, I would have wanted to help as well, but I had no idea what she could do at this point.

I glanced at Stan and he was smiling, staring at her.

"Let me help," Samantha said. "Anything. Sitting in that damn hotel room just waiting for something to happen is going to drive me crazy."

"Samantha," Stan said, before I could come up with some lame reason for it being important that she stay in the room. "I want you to focus on me for a moment, the sound of my voice."

Samantha turned toward Stan and nodded.

Suddenly Stan's right hand flew out as if to slap her in the face.

Samantha moved instantly, letting his open hand pass by her without touching her.

"I think she's ready to help you," Stan said, smiling at me.

"What did you do to me?" Samantha asked, clearly stunned at whatever was happening.

"I couldn't give you your sight back," Stan said, "so I just opened up your existing senses a little bit. You had already opened them a great deal since losing your vision. Now, just trust the information you are getting."

"I'm already used to doing that," she said. "Thank you, I think."

Stan laughed. "Don't mention it. It's not often I get to help someone who doesn't play poker."

Stan smiled at me. "I think she can help you now."

I nodded, believing him. After his little almost-slap demonstration, I had no doubt.

"Samantha, you come with me and Patty," I said. Then I glanced at Stan and Screamer. "We'll all meet out at the warehouse before six."

I noticed that even Stan nodded to that. I was hoping he was going to join us out there. Having a gambling god and all his powers along for the ride wouldn't hurt.

"Have a good lunch," Stan said, scooting his chair back and standing. "Nice meeting you, Samantha."

"Nice meeting you as well," Samantha said. "And thank you again, for whatever you did to me. It's amazing."

Suddenly, all the sounds of the restaurant pounded back in on the table like a wave hitting a beach. Madge moved toward us, a bubble half-popped in her mouth.

Stan was gone.

"Okay, someone tell me I'm not going completely nuts or dreaming," Samantha said.

"The gods do that to you," Screamer said, laughing. "They can drive you crazy."

"Gods?" Samantha asked.

"What can I get for you folks to eat?" Madge said, moving up and saving us from explaining to Samantha that there were levels of gods that existed that people prayed to all the time, but never really thought existed.

Madge stood close and towered over the table in a way I never wanted Madge to tower over me. It seemed as if the lights had gone dimmer in the restaurant. I looked up and could barely see Madge's forehead, her eyes, and the tip of her nose over her huge breasts.

I was in a breast eclipse. No wonder the lights had dimmed.

"Roast turkey sandwich," I said, staring at the menu instead of looking upward.

We all ordered and soon enough the light came back to the table as Madge turned and walked away.

Samantha giggled and whispered to Patty. "We're they as big as my enhanced senses told me they were?"

Patty nodded. "Bigger."

I started to glance at Madge as she walked away.

"Don't look," Screamer whispered to me.

It took every superpower I had, but I didn't.

••◆13◆••

THE BOOKKEEPER

AFTER LUNCH, Samantha had taken her dog Sue for a short walk and then back to her room and left Sue there. With whatever Stan had done to Samantha's four remaining senses, she had said she wasn't going to need Sue as much.

When Samantha came walking out of the side door to the Horseshoe with her sunglasses on, but acting and moving as if she could see everything, I was a believer.

After the three of us were in Patty's car, with Patty driving, me in the front seat, and Samantha in the back, Patty asked Samantha what the new senses felt like.

"Same as before," Samantha said, laughing. "I'm still smelling, hearing, feeling and tasting like before. It's just that the first three are very heightened, and the information I'm getting from the three senses of smelling, hearing, and feeling is being put together better in my head, forming pretty good images of things."

I turned my head to look at her and ask a question, but Samantha pointed a finger at me. "There, I can tell you turned your head and are looking at me." She reached forward and gently touched my cheek. "My combined senses even tell me exactly how far your face is from me."

"Like a computer putting data together and forming a composite," I said.

"Amazing," Patty said.

"It is," Samantha said. "This Stan person, whoever he was, did me a huge favor."

"And speaking of Stan," I said, turning to look at Patty as she headed the car out of the downtown area toward where I assumed The Bookkeeper lived. "How do you two know each other?"

She actually blushed a little.

"Oh, this might be a good story," Samantha said, laughing. "I don't need sight to tell she's blushing."

Patty actually blushed some more at that, then glanced at me, more than likely trying to get a read on how much I really wanted to know.

"Spit it out," I said, smiling at her.

"I met Stan about eighty years ago, at a club in a town called Garden City, up in Idaho. It was a gambling town on the edge of Boise at the time, full of nightclubs and card rooms and slot machines, before Idaho outlawed gambling of that type."

"Eighty years?" I said, staring at her, shocked. "That means you are one of the gods?"

"No, of course not," she said, smiling at me. "I'm at your level, only on the hotel management side. I help people who need help, just like you do."

"What do they call you?" I asked, smiling at her. "Front Desk Girl."

"Mostly just Patty," she said, laughing. "But I like that. I might use it."

"Explain the eighty years part," Samantha said from the back seat. "I have a sense you're only in your mid-thirties, not ninety or more."

"Yeah," I said. "I didn't know us superhero-types lived that long."

"No one's told you that yet, huh?" she said, smiling at me. "It's one of the benefits of the job. You're still new at this stuff. You'll learn."

The idea that I might live for a hundred years and look the same sort of stunned me. I just hadn't given getting old much thought, since in poker you get more respect if you look a little older and grizzled. I'd have to talk to Patty about this after we were done stopping the slot machines.

"So, do I even want to ask how old you really are?" Samantha said, "not that I'm going to believe any of this."

Patty smiled. "Always better to keep them guessing. Anyway, we're almost there."

"Nice avoidance on the Stan question," I said.

She just smiled at me while Samantha chuckled in the back seat.

I glanced out at the older-style ranch houses we were passing. Clearly Patty and Screamer had had dealings with this Bookkeeper person and didn't like him much.

"So who is this Bookkeeper?" Samantha asked before I could.

"He's a man who has spent his entire lifetime, and all his energy, working statistics. He sees patterns in things no one else does. He was granted longer life a hundred years back to keep studying in exchange for helping out in situations like this one."

"Everyone's not getting older," I said, shaking my head.

"I think I still am," Samantha said. "But at this point, I wouldn't even swear to that."

Both Patty and I laughed.

Then Patty said, "This guy is a real pig in just about every sense of the word. Don't let him get to you, because he enjoys that. If we stay focused on the slot machines, he'll be able to help us, I hope."

Patty stopped the car in front of a ranch-style house that needed painting and other repairs. All the windows had been boarded over from the inside, and there wasn't a live plant anywhere in the yard. The neighbors on both sides had put up tall fences to block out the sight as much as possible. Clearly, this was the one house that brought down the property values. There seemed to always be one in every neighborhood.

I couldn't talk much. I hated working on lawns and gardens more than just about anything besides going to a dentist. It was one of the reasons I lived in a double-wide mobile home in a mobile home park, where for a few extra bucks a month the owner of the park hired someone to keep the outside of my place looking at least decent.

We all climbed out into the hot afternoon. I was surprised at the intensity of the heat that hit my face after Patty's cool car. I moved to help Samantha, but it was clear she wasn't going to need my help. She got out easily, moved around the car, and expertly stepped up over the low curb and onto the sidewalk.

"This is going to be rough," Samantha said, turning to Patty and me. "I can smell this place clear out here."

All I could smell was the hot afternoon desert air.

"I can leave the car running and you can wait out here," Patty said. "If it's going to be too much for your new levels of senses."

"No, it will be fine," Samantha said. "I've got to learn to block some senses at times. Might as well be sooner than later. But I think all of us are going to need a shower after going in there."

I had a quick flash of the three of us standing naked together in a shower, then pushed the image aside. Samantha was married with a missing husband, Patty was a superhero. That sort of thing just wasn't going to happen.

"Let's get this over with," Patty said, starting up the front sidewalk that looked like it had been designed to weave in and around some sort of desert plants. But there were no plants, just gray gravel and dirt on both sides of the walk.

Samantha followed Patty and I brought up the rear.

Across the street, a neighbor peeked out of a closed curtain, and in the distance was the faint rumble of the freeway. Otherwise, this suburb was as quiet and dead as they came on a hot weekday afternoon.

Before Patty could even knock the door opened.

The man standing there was tiny, not more than five foot tall, with beady rat-eyes staring out over the tops of a thin pair of reading glasses. He had on gray, food-stained slacks and a dress shirt that might have been one color once, years before. For some reason, when Patty and Screamer had called this guy a pig, I had imagined him to be large and fat, not tiny and thin. He was bone thin, actually.

"Stan called ahead, told me you three were coming. Get in here before you let out all the cool air. Power doesn't come cheap, you know."

He turned away from the door, leaving it open for us to follow.

Patty shrugged and headed into the dark interior.

Samantha turned a little pale and followed, stumbling a little on the door step before regaining her balance.

A moment later I understood why she had stumbled. The smell coming from that open door was enough to gag a real pig. The smell was a cross between moldy cardboard, a backed-up toilet in a public restroom, and an un-emptied cat box. Samantha had been right, we were all going to need a shower after this.

I pushed the door closed and stopped waiting for my eyes to adjust to the dim light. The smell seemed to close down over me like a thick blanket. I had this instant desire to turn, open the door, and run for the street. But that wasn't an image of a superhero that I really wanted to give out. Superheroes dove in when all others ran. Patty and Samantha both were ahead of me, so I could make it as well.

With the door closed, it suddenly became very cool in the house, almost too cool. I could hear the sounds of a central air-conditioning system running from vents in the ceiling. The thing must have been turned up to full blast.

My eyes adjusted a little and I could see enough from the dim light coming from an adjacent room to tell the living room was packed to the ceiling with trash. And I do mean the ceiling, with stacks of paper, magazines, and books everywhere, forming a huge mound on both sides of the trail to the next room. I had read of a man in New York who had an apartment filled like this and a mound had collapsed on him and trapped him for two days.

I moved quickly down the canyon between walls of stacked paper, hoping against hope that I would brush nothing, that no stack would tumble onto me. Having Patty and a blind woman rescue me from a stack of paper might be more than my ego could handle.

I finally made it into the light area that must have been a dining room at one point. Now the entire room was filled with computers, monitors, and other electronic equipment. A big orange cat lay on the top of one computer, its tail flicking back and forth as it stared at me. So the cat explained one of the smells, the stacked paper and high air-conditioning explained the mold smell. That left the backed-up toilet smell which I had no intention of investigating.

The Bookkeeper was already in the high-backed chair in front of the computer, his fingers working over the keys as fast as I had ever seen anyone type. There were no other chairs, no place to even lean in the clutter, so the three of us just stood and watched him.

Actually, two of us watched him and Samantha did her other-senses thing.

After a long moment of typing he said, "I was wondering when you people would come talk to me. I had something like this happening projected years ago."

The man's voice was high and shrill, and even though he had said nothing really annoying, I felt annoyed at him anyway.

"You sent the note to the *Sun*?" I asked.

"Yeah," he said, still typing. "Had to get some of you idiots on the right track."

"And exactly what is the *right* track?" Patty asked, her voice low and very pointed.

Right at that moment, I decided I never wanted her angry at me. Not only did I have no idea what superpowers she had, the feeling of anger in her voice was enough to freeze this already cold house.

"Ghost slots," the little man said.

"We already knew that," I said. "We've already seen them in their home warehouse. What more can you help us with?"

"Well good for you," the little guy said, still typing while he looked up with a sneer on his rat-like face. Then, without looking he hit one key and pushed back. A moment later a high-speed printer spit out two sheets of paper. The little man handed the sheets to Patty.

"The exact times and locations the machines will appear over the next two days. That help?" He stared at me, daring me to say something.

I nodded at him, holding his gaze with mine. "A lot. So tell me, are there patterns in who these machines have been taking?"

"No," he said. "I've plugged in sixty-three names, including the name of this woman's husband."

He pointed to Samantha, then went on.

"No patterns in the victims."

"No one controlling them?" Patty asked.

The little man flicked the papers Patty was holding. "If there was outside control could I tell you when and where they were going to appear?"

"Not unless you knew who was controlling them."

"You're a funny man," he said, staring at me, his tiny black eyes seeming to dig right under my skin. "No one controls ghost slots, but they are machines and their actions can be predicted. If you aren't smart enough to stop them with that, I can't help you. Show yourselves out and close the door behind you tightly."

With that, he turned back to the computer screen and started typing.

"Contact Stan if you come up with something more," I said.

"There is nothing more."

Without another word, I led the way back through the towering stacks of paper and garbage to the front door.

Outside, I was hit in the face with a blast of hot, clean-smelling air. In all the years of being in and out of Las Vegas, I never thought I'd hear myself say I was glad to breathe the air there. But at that moment, any air besides the putrid cold air inside that house seemed like a drink from a mountain stream.

As Patty closed the door Samantha said, "Now I wish I had waited in the car."

Patty took her elbow and led her down the sidewalk toward the car.

"You going to be all right?" I asked as she slid into the back seat.

"If I don't throw up on the back of your head going into town, I'll be fine," she said.

Patty looked worried and Samantha just sat in the back seat looking green. I sat beside Patty, holding the two sheets of paper and staring at the locations of the future appearances of the ghost slots, not having a clue what to do next. I always figured that superheroes always came up with a plan after discovering important information.

I was plan-less.

At least I had another superhero beside me that might bail me out.

Halfway back to town I broke the silence and asked her. She had no idea what would be the best thing to do with the information either, besides giving it to the police.

Two plan-less superheroes and a nauseated blind woman. Not exactly the best team to save the entire casino industry and a whole bunch of people's lives.

··◆ *14* ◆··

THE TROOPS ARE GATHERED

I COULDN'T REMEMBER a shower that had felt so good. It was as if the smell from The Bookkeeper's house had stuck to me like a paste. I could almost see the water washing the smell off, sweeping it down the drain in a thick, gooey mess.

I stuffed the clothes I had been wearing into a plastic bag for hotel cleaning, and after I got out of the shower I called the front desk to come pick the bag up. I couldn't imagine leaving those clothes in my room.

I ran a wet wash cloth over my Poker Boy leather coat to clean it off both inside and out, then switched to a different hat, leaving the first one to air out beside the window. I still needed my superhero uniform for my powers to work, and no smell was going to stop that.

On the way down the elevator to the front desk area, I had this intense desire to just hit the second floor button, get off and go play some poker. I had come to Las Vegas for the tournament and hadn't done much more so far than just walk through the tournament area a few times.

Of course, I couldn't let the ghost slots keep taking people. I had the location of where they were going to show up next, and if The Bookkeeper was right, we could now at least save anyone new from getting taken.

Was Samantha's husband and the others who were taken still alive? Could these monsters be stopped? Those two questions alone were enough to get me right on past the World Series of Poker tournament area and down to the lobby.

I guess I was a superhero first, a poker player second.

Patty and Samantha were both standing near the front desk. Patty looked refreshingly clean, her skin almost glowing, the smile back on her fantastic face. She had her wet hair pulled back off her head, exposing my favorite mole. She had changed into black dress slacks and a Horseshoe employee's shirt that she had tucked in, shaping every wonderful thing about her body.

Her raspberry smell was strong enough to greet me like a hug as I joined them. She had said she was going to use the employee locker room to clean up. Clearly, she must have stashed a bottle of her favorite shampoo in her locker. Either that or the raspberry smell was just her natural smell. I was fine with either way.

Samantha also looked clean and freshly dressed in a tan blouse and skirt and sandals. She had on her black glasses, but none of her movements indicated she was blind in any respect. Stan's help with her other senses had given her back her freedom of movement completely.

"Feeling better?" I asked her.

"Still a touch green around the gills," she said. "But getting better by the moment."

"So it's proven," Patty said as we all turned and headed out the door and into the warm afternoon heat. "Men do take longer in showers. I even had time to make copies of the list we got."

She handed me a copy.

"I didn't know it was a race," I said, giving her my best disarming smile. "But under the right kind of pressure I can be pretty darned fast with a bar of soap."

Samantha snorted, but Patty just smiled at me and said nothing. I had no idea what she was thinking at that moment. She was impossible for me to read in any fashion.

Right at that moment, I would have traded a bunch of my superpowers for Johnny and Geneva's ability to be hooked up to Patty in thought. I could only hope that Patty was thinking of me in the shower, in a *nice* way.

The image of Patty in the shower with me, handing me the soap with that smile of hers made me trip over the curb and stumble.

"You all right?" Patty asked as she moved around her car.

I nodded, not trusting myself to say anything at that moment. Every time I turned around, this wonderful woman was surprising me, making me stumble, making me have wonderfully rude thoughts about her. I couldn't remember the last time a woman had had this kind of effect on me.

Maybe it was the raspberry.

Maybe it was one of her superpowers. I sure hoped to find out at some point, after all this was over.

With me in the co-pilot seat and Samantha in the back, Patty expertly drove her car out the old Boulder Highway toward the warehouse where the ghost slots lived. The next location The Bookkeeper said the slots would show was in an old casino out on the same highway at a little after seven this evening.

I planned on giving a copy of the list to Johnny so that he could have the area in that casino guarded to keep anyone else from being taken. But I really hoped to find a way to stop the machines before then.

We rode in silence through a few stop lights, then Samantha asked, "Do you think Ben is still alive?"

Patty glanced up into the rearview mirror, then at me.

I turned as much as my seat belt would let me turn to face Samantha. "I don't honestly know," I said. "What does your gut tell you?"

"That he is," Samantha said.

"Trust that feeling," Patty said.

"I agree," I said. "There're a lot of things in this world that happen and are not easily explained. One is the connection between a couple in love. It's as powerful a sense as the ones you are using to *see* without your eyes. Let that feeling come forward and you'll know your answer."

Samantha was nodding, clearly lost inside her own head.

"The connection is real," Patty said. "If you know he's still alive, then he is."

"Thank you," Samantha said, her voice quivering a little. "And thank you both for helping me."

"It's what we do," Patty said as she accelerated the car away from a stop light, weaving through traffic like an expert.

I turned back around to watch the road ahead. The last thing I needed at this point was to get motion sickness. A car-sick superhero wasn't going to be much good to anyone. Facing backward in a car always made me carsick, even one being driven as smoothly as Patty was driving.

The clock on Patty's dashboard said ten minutes until five. We were going to be an hour early for the six o'clock gathering. I hoped Stan and Screamer would both show up early as well. The information they had gone after was going to be critical in how we stopped these machines. We needed to get the machines to spit back out the people it had taken, or find where they had been taken to, then figure out what was powering the slots, and how to turn them off.

I had no clear idea how any of this was going to work, but my sense was to trust the team and it would all come together.

In the warehouse parking lot the only car was a marked police car sitting directly in front of the door. When Patty pulled up and stopped, one of the officers climbed out and walked toward the car.

Patty put her window down, letting in a blast of warm air. She smiled at the officer. "I'm Patty Ledgerwood."

She indicated me, then Samantha. "This is Conway Moore, and Samantha MacDuff."

The officer nodded. "Detective State says you have clearance to go in. He's on his way here. Should be arriving in less than ten minutes."

Patty glanced at me, then smiled at the officer. "We'll wait for him out here."

"I'll tell him," the officer said, then turned and headed back for his car as Patty slid up her window and turned up the air conditioning to cool the car quickly.

"Nice in here," Stan said from the back seat.

"Cripes!" Samantha said as Patty and I spun around to see Stan sitting next to Samantha in the back seat.

"Ring a bell or something next time," Samantha said, both her hands on her chest. "Not sure if my heart can handle that again."

Stan laughed. "Sorry about that."

For the first time, I actually thought that moving up the ranks to one of the gods might be a good idea. Stan's ability to pop in and out and move around without cars and planes would sure save a lot of time and money. I could play in the World Series and sleep at nights in my own bed. But I doubted the trade-off would be worth the politics and infighting that went on among the gods.

"How are the enhanced senses working for you?" Stan asked Samantha.

"Perfectly," Samantha said. "I hope you're not going to take them away after we solve all this."

Stan laughed. "Of course not. But we may ask you to help us once in a while in trade."

"That's a deal I can live with," Samantha said.

"Power?" I asked Stan. "Any idea what is powering those ghost slots?"

"Nothing from this plain of existence," Stan said. "Bernie in maintenance tried to trace the power from the things in there, but couldn't do it. It's like the power circles back in from inside."

Bernie was the gambling god in charge of casino maintenance and operations. I had heard his nickname was Back-up Bernie.

"So shutting the power off to those things from the outside isn't an option," Patty said.

"Afraid not," Stan said.

"Something about that circling thing," I said, releasing my seat belt so I could turn and face Stan in the back. "Any chance the power is coming from the people it has taken."

"You mean like the myth says?" Patty asked.

I nodded.

"Possible," Stan said. "Bernie couldn't find any yes or no on that either. This has got him as stumped as the rest of us."

I hated it when gods said they were stumped. It made me feel even less capable of saving Samantha's husband and all the rest. What could a minor superhero do that the gods couldn't do?

"Sorry I couldn't be of more help," Stan said. "Good luck in there."

"You're not coming in with us?" I asked, but by the time my question reached the back seat, Stan was gone.

"Someone's got to put a bell on him," Samantha said. "So he can warn us when he's coming and going."

"So the gods are as clueless as we are at this point," Patty said, turning to look at me with those big brown eyes of hers. "Any ideas?"

"A few," I said.

I didn't add that all my really great ideas concerned her naked in a shower and me holding the soap.

I didn't have a clue what to do about the ghost slot machines, saving over seventy lives, and stopping the ruin of the entire gambling industry.

"Great," she said. "Because I sure don't."

At that moment, Johnny and Geneva drove up beside Patty's car and stopped, followed closely by Screamer's car. It seemed it was time to get to work and do some superhero-type deeds, if I could just figure out which deeds we needed to do.

··◆ *15* ◆··

A (SORT OF) PLAN FORMS

ALL SEVEN OF US moved into the warehouse and stood just inside the door in a large circle, surrounded by thousands of dead slot machines.

The place was warm, but not as hot as outside, and it echoed, giving all of our voices a feedback quality. The warehouse smelled of dry dust with a faint burnt electrical odor over everything. The big space would have given me the creeps even without the ghost slot machines living back along the side wall.

Patty stood beside me on my right, Samantha on my left.

Johnny and Geneva stood across from me. Both had occasional looks in their eyes as if listening to something in the distance. They weren't touching, but if I had my guess, their power to hear each others thoughts didn't need touch anymore.

Screamer stood to Patty's right with a grunge-looking man with long hair black pulled back, a nose ring, and tattoos showing on most areas of bare skin, including a naked woman along his neck that twisted and moved every time the guy turned his head. He wore jeans and a loose shirt and looked like he hadn't had a good meal in years. He carried a beat-up blue backpack in one hand and an unlit cigarette in the other.

Screamer had introduced him as Brian, but said everyone just called him Tech, since he was so good with computers and machines.

I had expected Screamer to bring an older man, someone who had actually worked on the old-style slot machines back before everything went computers. But if Screamer thought this guy could do the job, then he could do it.

I started off by asking Johnny and Geneva what they had discovered. They gave a quick rundown of how they had eliminated any last thoughts of this being a magic trick, then told us about their meeting with Rees, a major magician, often finishing each other's sentences as they spoke.

"Wow," Tech said, staring at Geneva and Johnny. "You actually talked with Rees "The Mechanic" in his home?"

"Yeah," Johnny said, clearly half-disgusted at the question.

"He's the best there is, man," Tech said.

"So anything come of the meeting with him?"

"Just that he was surprised about the people being taken when the machine is showing a jackpot," Geneva said.

"Real surprised," Johnny said.

"You sure on that jackpot part?" Tech asked Geneva.

Both her head and Johnny's nodded like they were being pulled by the same string.

"Rees said that being taken, actually losing on jackpots just isn't the way the machines work."

"What's that mean?" Screamer asked Tech about a half second before I could ask him the same question. The security tape we saw of the machine taking Ben out of the Horseshoe wasn't set at such an angle that we could see the reels on the face of the machine Ben was playing.

"Man, it means that someone got inside those old things and reset a half-dozen different settings on the reel board."

"So someone is behind this after all?" Johnny asked.

"No kidding," Tech said. "No other way a machine can get set like that. Can't happen accidentally that's for sure."

"Why's that?" I asked, wanting to be very sure.

Tech stared at me for a moment. "There's a solenoid on the reel board that works like a switch to determine jackpots. I don't even think a normal solenoid in one of these old sixties machines has a setting for full payout every time. There wouldn't be enough coins in the machine for one, and second there would be no reason to even have such a setting designed in. No, this is special work here by someone."

I wasn't sure I understood exactly what he meant, but I nodded and let it go for the moment.

Johnny indicated we should hold on a second, then pulled out his cell phone and made a quick call. When someone answered he identified himself, asked for a Captain Walk, then said, "Captain, I've got a lead on the disappearances. I need someone to get the records from Standard Slots on anyone granted access to the old Valley Slots graveyard warehouse."

He listened for a moment, then said, "Just the last month should be enough. Thanks."

I nodded to him as he clicked his cell phone shut, then turned back to Tech. "So how do we change those settings back?"

"And get my husband out of that thing," Samantha said. "If that's where he's at."

Tech shrugged, causing the naked woman on his neck to contort into a very unnatural posture. "I figure we first got to check out what's powering the whole mess, shut that off. Do that and I can open up the machine and reset everything, maybe replace that faulty solenoid.

I stared at him. I had seen those machines come and go, once on a tape, once up close. I couldn't imagine anyone simply walking up to one of them and opening the front.

"Are we going to need a key to open the things?" Screamer asked.

Tech held up his old backpack. "Got that, buddy."

"In case we can't stop these things quickly," Patty said to Johnny, "You need to get some people at these locations at these times."

She handed Johnny a copy of the sheets that The Bookkeeper had given us showing where the machines were going to appear next.

"You found out who is controlling these things?" Geneva asked, glancing at the paper in Johnny's hand as he read it.

"No," Patty said, "but we know who sent your newspaper that first note. A guy called The Bookkeeper who uses math to predict these things."

"And you are sure he has nothing to do with this?" Johnny asked.

"Completely," I said.

Johnny nodded. "So we have about two hours until the machines shift, if this is to be believed. So what do we do next?"

"I suppose we see if Tech and I can get the face of one of those things open."

At that moment Johnny's cell phone rang and he answered it, listening for a moment before saying, "You're sure?"

He listened again for a short moment, with the rest of us standing there in the warehouse staring at him.

Then he said "Thanks."

He clicked his phone closed and shook his head. "The last man to be in this warehouse was almost three weeks ago. A guy named Harry Timmer."

"Oh, man," Tech said. "Old Harry's been missing for three weeks."

"That's what my Captain just said."

"You know him?" Screamer asked.

"Sure," Tech said. "Everyone in the business knows old Harry. He's a retired slot tech from the days before computers took over the machines. He liked working on the old mechanicals, fixing them up and selling them as novelty items. He was always scrounging for parts. Made some good money doing it too."

"So he'd know how to reset the slots?" Johnny asked.

Tech laughed. "He could make those old machines dance if he wanted. But, man, if you're thinkin' he's behind all this, you've flat lost it. Old Harry wouldn't hurt a fly, let alone use the machines he loved for something like taking people."

"Maybe he was forced to," Johnny said.

Tech shook his head, making the woman on his neck dance the twist. "I can't see him doing this."

"So let's go take a look at these things," I said. "Johnny, you and I will take off the tarp. Tech, you see what you can see, but don't touch them just yet."

"Got you it in one on that," Tech said.

I led the group to the far aisle and down toward the ghost slots. I could see faint colors coming from under the tarp, pulsing like a warning light. And the closer we got, the closer I wanted to get, as their unnatural attraction was pulled at me even through the tarp.

Patty, Geneva, Samantha and Screamer stopped about twenty paces from the machines, leaving Johnny and me and Tech walking slowly at the machines like three old-west marshals headed toward a gunfight.

I could feel the pull of the things getting stronger with every step. A little voice in my head was telling me to sit down, just play a little.

What could it hurt?

Tech stopped across the aisle facing the slots and stood waiting as I went to the far side of the machines and carefully grabbed the tarp without touching any metal.

Johnny did the same on his side and then nodded at me.

"Now," I said.

We both yanked at the same time, pulling the tarp down and away.

The entire warehouse again lit up with the rainbow of colors coming off the glowing Saturn Slots. The things seemed to have so much energy that they were pulsing.

"Oh, man," Tech said, stepping back.

"Cripes," Screamer said.

The moment the tarp was gone the pull to sit down and play was fantastically stronger. I could feel myself struggling with the desire. And I had no doubt I wasn't the only one feeling it as Geneva stepped forward and took hold of Johnny's arm and drew him a few steps back.

Over the years as Poker Boy I had run into my share of things I wanted to just run away from. But as a superhero, I just had never done that. I guess running scared just wasn't part of the job description. But that said, right at that moment, I wanted to run as fast and as far from those machines as I could get. However, I think I was so scared my feet didn't want to move.

So I just stared at the machines, at the blinking lights, at the bright colors, at the incredible image of Saturn and its rings dominating the area over the machines and the four wooden chairs.

I took a deep breath and dug down deep into what made me a good poker player. I had been stared-down by the best players in the world, bluffed and intimidated, yet I had always remained cool and level, no matter how much money had been at stake.

Now there was something a lot more than money at stake. People's lives. This was not the time for Poker Boy to break.

So I stared back at the four machines, daring them to take me down, daring them to get to me or anyone else around me.

After a moment, I realized I had won. My mind had done its trick of putting things into compartments, just like it did with the fear I felt on the final tables of big tournaments. The force the machines were using to try to draw me to them was now trapped off to one side of my mind. It was still there, but it wasn't going to affect what I did, how I played this hand.

Maybe being able to do that was also one of my superpowers. If it was I was going to have to figure out a name for it. Something like my Fear-Away Power.

I glanced around at the others.

Johnny and Geneva were also doing fine it seemed, keeping each other level.

Screamer had a confused look on his face, like he was hearing something in the distance. I had no idea how the pull on these machines would affect his power.

Patty tried a half-smile at me. It was enough to show me she was fine as well. As Front Desk Girl, I was sure she had dealt with more angry people than I had. More than likely, she had a way of compartmentalizing this type of energy like I had. Maybe her own special superpower.

Tech was still standing facing the machines, but his look had changed from fear and shock to curiosity. It seemed the fearlessness of youth was serving him well.

"Ben's in there," Samantha said, moving toward the machines like she was a zombie in a bad movie. "I can sense him. He's trapped in there."

I stepped across the front of the machines and took her by the shoulders, stopping her five paces from the machines beside Johnny and Geneva. "What do you mean you can sense him?"

"He's in there," she said.

Everything about her seemed locked on the machines. She clearly wasn't aware of where she was at the moment for some reason. She half struggled against me, but I wouldn't let her take another step toward those monsters.

"How do you know?" Johnny asked her, stepping up and blocking her from the machines.

With that she seemed to come back to the warehouse, back to a presence in her own body.

She turned to face me. "My new senses," she said, clearly checking in with herself.

"New senses?" Johnny asked.

"She's blind," I said to Johnny, "so Stan at lunch gave her other senses, some extra power so that she could help us out. She's just getting used to them."

"Stan?" Geneva asked.

"Long story," I said, not wanting to waste time right at that point explaining gambling gods to someone who wasn't going to understand. "Just believe that like you two, she has some special senses."

Both Geneva and Johnny again nodded as one.

"So what did you sense?" I asked Samantha.

"Still sensing," she said. "Ben is close. He's in that machine and very much alive. I can tell he's confused and a little angry and getting slowly tired."

"Is his energy being drained?" Patty asked. She had moved up to stand beside Samantha.

Samantha nodded slowly. "Maybe. He's getting tired."

Patty glanced at me. "The myth."

I nodded, agreeing. The power was more than likely coming from the people inside. And for the first time in some time I had an idea on how to solve this problem. Samantha held the solution to what we were facing. If she could somehow link to her husband and transfer that information to me, I might be able to figure out what to do next.

"Screamer," I said, motioning for him to come up beside us.

"Samantha, you know how Screamer put the images of what Patty saw into your mind?"

"You want him to put what I'm sensing into yours?" Samantha said.

"If you don't mind."

"Anything to help Ben get out of there," she said, the strength in her voice clear and strong, now that she believed her husband was alive.

I glanced at Screamer and he nodded his agreement. He touched my arm, then Samantha's arm.

For a moment everything went black, as if someone had turned out the lights in a windowless room. Then I realized what I was experiencing was Samantha's blindness.

I opened my mind up to the other senses, amazed at how the warehouse around me came back into focus in sort of an overlay with what I was seeing with my own eyes, only vastly enhanced.

I could see the heat of each person, smell them, hear even their stomach's rumbling. And all the thousands of sensory inputs were coming together to form a picture without color, yet very clear and accurate.

I also suddenly knew Samantha's memories, her fears, everything about her, and I had no doubt she knew everything about me.

"Can you hear him?" Samantha asked.

"Yes," Screamer said.

I realized there was a person, a presence I didn't recognize from my own world, yet was very, very familiar to Samantha. I could see what she meant by sensing him. He was there, inside the machine.

Ben was alive.

All the people that had been taken were alive. I could sense that as well. They were existing in the wires, in the circuits of that machine. To them it felt like white corridors, forever twisting around on each other, with no exit. Most of them seemed to be walking those white corridors, getting more and more tired.

Of the four machines, it seemed that only the one on the right had been taking people. They were all in there. I somehow just knew that fact.

"Can you communicate with Ben?" Johnny asked from a place that seemed outside the world I was focused on. Part of my mind was in the white spaces of the circuits of the machine, part of my mind was still aware of the warehouse, with Samantha's heightened senses as an overlay.

I felt Samantha try to contact her husband. I felt her mind call out to him.

But Ben didn't respond, didn't hear her.

Screamer let go of both of us, breaking the image of the white place where the people were trapped.

Breaking my contact with Samantha's enhanced hearing and smells and feelings. It was as if I had suddenly gone from a full color movie to a black-and-white one. It was shocking the difference in attention to other senses rounded out the world around a person.

"You all right?" Screamer asked Samantha.

She nodded. "Ben can't hear us. But he's in there. All of the people are."

I glanced at Screamer and he nodded in agreement.

"Can you talk to him," Johnny asked. "Get those inside to shut down the machine?"

"No," I said.

That way was a dead-end. But I was getting a glimmering of a plan.

"Tech," I said, "anything you can do to open those things up?"

"I don't see why not," he said. "But I'd be afraid to do anything unless I was completely sure what I was doing would kick those people out of there."

"I agree with you there," I said. "Your friend Harry seems to be the first to have disappeared in there. If you could talk to him, you think the two of you might come up with something?"

"Him on the inside, me out here?" Tech said. "Sure."

I nodded and turned to look at Johnny.

"I'll do it," both Johnny and Geneva said at the exact same moment.

"Do what?" Samantha asked.

"Stick a nickel in that thing and go inside to find Harry," I said.

"That's bug-nuts crazy," Tech said.

"Oh, no," Samantha said.

Patty just looked pale.

Screamer shook his head.

The silence in the warehouse was smothering.

··◆16◆··

CONTACT AT TWENTY-FOUR VOLTS

I STARED AT JOHNNY as he watched through Geneva's eyes what was happening in the casino with the ghost slots. At one point he had shouted "Get her out of there!"

Then he had laughed and explained to all of us standing there staring at him, worried, that an old woman had sat down at the ghost slots. He said that Patty and Geneva and a cop had managed to stop the woman before she got a coin into the slot. His laughing and shaking his head cut the tension a little in the warehouse among the five of us.

Screamer and I stood next to Johnny, ready to help him in any way we could under the circumstances.

"Geneva's sitting down at the machine," he said.

Suddenly he was very serious again and I could hear the worry in his voice and see it on his face.

He didn't like this, and I didn't much like it either, but it had come to be our best choice.

And our only plan.

Tech was afraid to touch the machine for fear he would do something that would kill all the people inside. He wanted the help of the old guy I was betting had reset the slots in the first place, Harry Timmer. But Harry was inside the slots, and had been from the start. So someone had to go in and talk to old Harry and relay the information out to Tech.

The connection between Geneva and Johnny made one of them a natural for the job. I didn't like it, but none of us could come up with another way of trying to rescue all those people inside there.

As Geneva said to one of my objections, "You often have to jump into water and endanger yourself to rescue a drowning person."

She was right. I knew she was right. I just didn't much like the pool she was jumping into. And neither did anyone else.

"She's put a coin in and pulled the handle," Johnny said.

Suddenly he grabbed his head and bent forward, as if he had a bad hangover.

Screamer was about to grab him to hold him up, but I waived him off. Whatever was happening to Geneva and Johnny, I didn't want Screamer feeling it as well.

Johnny moaned a few seconds later, but remained standing, bent over, his hands grabbing the sides of his head like he was trying to hold his skull together.

Then he screamed.

It was like no scream I could have ever imagined coming from a big, powerful detective. It sounded like a combination of him and Geneva, high and sharp at the same time as low and guttural. It sent chills up my spine.

The scream echoed through the warehouse, then Johnny tipped forward onto his hands and knees on the concrete.

"Help him!" Samantha said.

"Don't touch him yet," I said, waiving everyone away. "We need his connection with Geneva clear."

A moment later the slots shimmered into view, bringing back with them the intense desire to go sit down and just try my luck. But of course, putting a nickel in that slot machine at this point wouldn't have much luck involved. Just stupidity, which was how I often felt about playing slot machines even when they weren't ghost slots.

Around us, the gray of the warehouse had changed back to reflected colors and energy from the lights on the machine. Every face, every old slot machine covered in gray dust now had multiple colors as the image of Saturn glowed brighter than any light in the warehouse.

Being careful to not touch any of Johnny's skin to jeopardize his connection with Geneva, I bent down and he let me help him to his feet.

"What happened?" Screamer asked.

Johnny took a deep breath. "The shock and the pain knocked her out."

"Shock shouldn't have been that bad," Tech said. "Those machines are run on twenty-four volts."

"You all right?" I asked. I could feel his shoulders shaking a little, but with each passing second he seemed to be gaining control.

He nodded slowly. "I think so, but I'm betting on one hell of a headache."

"Is Geneva all right?" Samantha asked.

Again he nodded slowly. "I think so. She's knocked out, but I can still hear her thoughts under her dreams."

"Okay, now that's got to be real weird," Tech said.

I had to agree with Tech on that one. Listening to a person's dreaming mind must seem like watching a bad psychedelic movie while being very drunk.

"Actually, at the moment, she's dreaming she's swimming to the surface of a pool," Johnny said, his eyes staring off into the distance. "Very peaceful, no panic or worries. Hang on. I see what she's doing. She's trying to reach the surface and wake up."

We all stared at him until he finally nodded and turned to look at me. "She's all right. She's awake and she's in there."

He pointed to the ghost slot machine.

"Oh, wow, cool," Tech said. "What's it look like?"

"White corridors," Johnny said. "Everything is shades of white, including her clothing, hair and skin. All the colors are gone from everything. She feels normal-sized and very lost in the maze of corridors. Nothing seems to have any corners either, including the corridors. They're more like round tubes that twist and move off in different directions."

"I'll bet she's in the electrical wiring," Tech said. "Have her move until she finds a junction area and then describe it."

"She agreed," Johnny said.

"Is she meeting some of the others in there?"

"She is," Johnny said. "And she's already asking for Harry."

We all stood silent for a moment watching Johnny, who was with Geneva inside the ghost slots. After a moment, Johnny said, "It's weird, because I'm in there with her, and she's out here with me at the same time. It's helping her stay calm being here through my eyes. Also weird that everyone in there that she meets somehow knows they are inside a machine."

I had no idea how people trapped as energy inside the wiring of a machine could know where they were. I couldn't imagine there being windows out of the side of the wiring. But at this point, nothing about ghost slots would surprise me.

"Tech, she's at an intersection," Johnny said. "One corridor into a wide triangle area, three corridors out side-by-side."

Tech seemed to think for a minute, then said, "I'm betting she's at the electrical junction sending power to the wheels. You need to have her turn around and go back the way she came."

"You think you might know where Harry is at?" I asked Tech, surprised at how definite he sounded.

"If I was stuck in there, and knew where I was, I'd be at the solenoid on the reel board."

"Solenoid?" Patty asked as she came back toward us down the rows of dead slot machines. "Sounds like she's in there and just fine."

"She is," I said.

The relief on Patty's face was clear.

I was very happy to see her back from the casino. I felt more comfortable with her beside me on this problem. It was as if I got a "balance energy" from her, keeping my mind clear. Next time I made the final table of a big tournament, I might ask her to come and watch from the stands, just for that energy boost.

"The solenoid is an electric coil used as a control and switching devise," Tech said. "Its purpose is setting payouts on the machines built in this period. It's located on what they called the reel board, the electrical panel area that controls the three reels of the machine."

Patty stopped right beside me as I asked Tech the next logical question. "Is that one of the things that would have had to have been changed to make the machines hit jackpots all the time?"

"The main thing," Tech said.

"Hang on," Johnny said, holding his hands up. "Someone Geneva just ran into knows Harry."

There was a pause as we all waited for Johnny's next statement. Then he smiled at me. "Says he's been trying to help Harry figure out a way to escape. He's taking Geneva to Harry now."

"Great!" I said.

I turned to Screamer. "I'm going to need you to hook up Tech and Johnny, so Tech can talk directly to Harry. Make sure he gets everything right. Can you do that?"

"Easy," Screamer said.

"Hang on," Tech said, "you're saying that I can talk through Johnny, then through Geneva, to Harry who is inside that machine?"

"Actually, through me first," Screamer said, smiling at the young guy with all the tattoos.

"A conversation through three heads," Tech said. "I'm going to be lucky to not need counseling after this is finished."

I agreed with him on that. Running around in Samantha's head earlier had left me unsettled. I knew way too many things about her that I wanted to forget. Too much about her dreams, her fights with her husband, her sexual pleasures. And she knew the same stuff about me, which I didn't really want to think about.

I wasn't sure how Johnny and Geneva had made a constant connection between them work so quickly over the last day, but after my short romp with Samantha's mind, I now knew that I didn't want to see what Patty was thinking, or even know how she felt about me. And I didn't want her seeing my daydreams about her in the shower and me with a bar of raspberry soap. It was going to be a lot better learning about her slowly, blindly, one question at a time, one nude shower at a time.

More fun, too.

"She's almost to where Harry is at," Johnny said.

"Ready?" I asked Screamer.

"As I'll ever be."

I motioned for Tech to come over closer to Johnny while Scream-er placed himself between the two. Samantha and I and Patty stepped back out of the way.

"Here we go," Screamer said, winking at me.

Then he reached out and first touched Tech's arm, right below a tattoo of an eagle, then touched Johnny's arm.

Tech's worry left his face as his eyes sort of glazed over. Clearly he wasn't seeing the aisle of the old slot machine warehouse anymore. He was inside the slots, inside Geneva's mind.

Screamer looked at me, clearly in his eyes and reported what he was seeing. "Harry's sitting down in there. He seems very, very tired and old. I think the energy drain caused by the machine is almost too much for him.

"Yeah, it's me, Harry," Tech said out loud.

Screamer smiled and sort of rolled his eyes, making it clear to us that he thought it funny that some people had to talk when thinking to another person.

"Don't ask," Tech said. "I don't even understand how this works."

All of us smiled at that.

"I've been feeling that same way," Samantha whispered to Patty.

"So what did you do?" Tech asked the unseen Harry.

A moment later Tech said, "Oh, shit."

None of us smiled at that.

Screamer almost whispered to us, "Harry said he was the one that caused this all to happen, and he's very sorry."

"You're kidding?" Tech said. "You know how much pain and worry and fear you've caused."

A long pause followed that.

"So any idea exactly how many people are in here?" Tech asked.

Pause.

"So what's going to reverse this?"

Nothing for a moment. Screamer seemed to be listening and had stopped reporting to us the other side of the conversation.

"If it's that easy, how come you haven't done it before now?" Tech asked.

A very long pause that seemed to make the silence of the warehouse grow in intensity and power.

"Oh," Tech said.

"Oh, shit," Screamer said. He looked like he was about to be very sick.

"Impossible," Johnny said, shaking his head, the look of worry and fear very strong in his face.

"I'll be back," Tech said, then pulled his arm away from Screamer and staggered a few paces away.

Screamer let go of Johnny and turned to walk a few paces away.

Johnny just slumped to the concrete floor and put his head in his hands.

I glanced at the very worried look on Patty's face, then stepped forward toward Tech. "What happened. What was that all about?"

"No problem reversing the process Harry started," Tech said, staring at the floor without looking up at me. "Harry got sucked into these ghost slots while scrounging in here for parts. He figured he could reconfigure the machines from the inside to spit him back out, but he missed a setting, reversed a few things, and got the machines taking more people on jackpots."

"So he's the reason this has all happened?" I asked.

"Yeah, Harry trying to save himself caused all this," Screamer said, turning back to face me. "No wonder no one could figure out what was going on, or who was behind it."

Tech nodded. "He's feeling damn bad about it, too. And he has since figured out how to solve the problem and set the machines from in there to spit out everyone."

"So why hasn't he done that?" Samantha asked, moving up beside me. "Why hasn't he let my Ben out of there?"

"One chair," Patty said.

I turned and glanced at her, then at the one old wooden chair attached to the front of the Saturn slot machine that held everyone. She was right. Where would the people go?

"One chair," Screamer said, agreeing. "There are one hundred and three people in that machine right now counting Geneva and Harry. They would all appear in that chair, reformed in their bodies, like coins dropping out of a pay-out chute. About three per second."

"Not possible," Samantha said.

"That's right," Johnny said from where he sat on the floor. "They would all be killed, their bodies materialized together in a massive pile of flesh and bones."

"And there's no way to slow it down?" Samantha demanded.

"There is no setting in the machine that regulates the rate of pay-out," Tech said. "Just the amount."

"So get Harry to set the payout at one," I said.

Again Tech shook his head. "That's what Harry has been working on, but again, there are no single unit payouts on this machine, and nothing goes that low in any setting he can find. And if he can't find it from in there, it doesn't exist."

"How many is the minimum?" Patty asked.

"Three," Tech said. "Three, two, one-hundred. It's not going to matter."

I stared at the single chair in front of the old slot machine and tried to imagine three human bodies appearing there in one second. Tech was right. Three or one hundred. They would all die.

And die horribly.

··◆ *17* ◆··

TWO SUPERHEROES, NO SOAP

THE SILENCE in the big warehouse became intense as we all were lost in our own thoughts. It was as if we were sitting in a big, neon-lit tomb, the gray and dust of the place pushed back and barely held at bay by the bright colors of the enemy machines.

The pull from the ghost slots was still strong, but I had put the feeling off to one side and was ignoring it, and it seemed the rest were dealing with it as well, although none of us got within four paces of the things.

Over one hundred people were trapped in that one ghost slot machine, and there was no way to get them out safely. That fact was enough to depress just about anyone. And I couldn't even imagine how Johnny was feeling. He shared his mind with Geneva, and she was going to die with him inside her head. More than likely it would kill him as well, or do so much damage as to never let him function normally again.

I couldn't let that happen. There had to be a way to save them. There had to be.

We just had to find it.

I glanced around at the team. Johnny was sitting on the concrete floor. He was the closest to the machine, staring at it, clearly in contact with Geneva.

Samantha sat cross-legged a few feet behind him, her back against a tarp-covered machine.

Screamer was pacing up and down and up and down the aisle, his steps silent on the concrete floor.

Tech had walked twenty feet away and now stood with his back to everyone, not moving.

Patty stood beside me, her beautiful head tipped back as if she were studying something up near the roof of the big warehouse.

I moved over beside Johnny and knelt down. "How long does Geneva think they have in there?"

"Harry's been in there the longest and he's very weak," Johnny said. "There are a few others like him."

"Thanks," I said, standing and letting Johnny and Geneva go back to being together in their minds.

Not only was the town about to explode with the news of all the missing people, but if Harry died in there, drained of energy by the machine, there would be no chance at all of any rescue without sending Tech or someone else inside to set the machine.

I moved back over beside Patty and tapped her shoulder. She looked at me with those big brown eyes of hers and I almost forgot that I wanted to talk to her. I indicated that she should follow me toward the warehouse door. She nodded and without a word to any of the others we moved away.

I didn't exactly know what I wanted to talk to her about. She was a superhero like I was, had been around a lot longer than I had been, and she kept me balanced. If I was going to think out loud about this project, it made sense to think out loud to her. And right now, I really needed to do some out-loud thinking.

On really tough cases, like this one, I usually went back to my room, paced and talked to myself, trying to work out a solution. Granted, that wasn't the way I did things on a poker table, where I solved problems silently, without even showing emotion on my face unless I wanted the emotion shown. But this was a lot more serious than a poker tournament. Lives were at stake and I didn't need to keep my emotions hidden.

From the light coming in the open door, it was clear that the sun was starting to set. I could feel that the heat outside was still pretty intense from the way it poured in the open door. More than likely the heat wouldn't fade until closer to midnight.

Patty and I stopped and faced each other near the door. At that moment, as if I were playing a hand I was unsure of and was suddenly convinced my play was right, I knew what to say.

"Time," I said. "Time is our problem."

Patty nodded. "Three people per second materializing into the same space. It doesn't give us enough time to get each person out of the way before the next person starts to appear."

"Exactly," I said, now seeing one possible solution. "So we stop time between each person."

Patty stared at me like I had said something really silly, then slowly smiled. "Can you do that?"

I shrugged. "Stan told me I could do it when I needed to do it. But I have never needed to try, to be honest. And he can do it as well."

Patty sort of looked off into space for a second, then said, "I have the ability to stretch time for myself," she said. "It doesn't really stop, but it stretches for me so I can get a lot of paperwork done for customers and make it seem fast to them."

"Can you control that?"

"Sort of," she said. "Normally, it just sort of clicks-in, if you know what I mean."

"I do," I said. "Most of my powers are the same way. Sometimes I can bring them on with really intense focus, but usually they are just there when I need them."

"Me too," Patty said.

"Well, we need them now," I said. "Can you stretch time with me included?"

She looked worried, the first time I had ever seen a worried look on her face. "I can try."

She reached out and took my hand. For a moment I thought I heard the Hallelujah Chorus sung by a one-hundred member choir with me singing the lead. Her skin was as soft, as firm, and wonderful as I had imagined it would be. The image of her holding my hand while we stood naked in a shower flashed over my mind and I let myself go with the image for a moment before I realized what I was doing.

Somehow, I dropped the bar of raspberry soap, pushed the thoughts back, took a deep breath, and focused on the situation. Luckily I had that kind of control as a poker player, otherwise I might have pulled her into my arms and kissed her right there.

But I had control.

Control.

Control.

I repeated the word a few times more and was solidly back in the warehouse holding Patty's hand as she tried to slow down time around us.

"I think it's working," she said, smiling at me.

I glanced around. Where we were at near the door there was no way of telling. Nothing was moving in the slot machine graveyard.

"Can you hold it until we get back near the others?"

"I think so," she said. "Just don't let go of my hand. You're giving me energy I don't normally feel."

I didn't tell her what energy she was giving me. I figured that would be more appropriate later, after we rescued everyone.

Hand-in-hand, like two school kids, we walked back to the aisle with the ghost slots and the rest of the team. No one there seemed to be moving, but they hadn't been moving much before we left either.

Then Patty pointed at Screamer and smiled.

I could see what she was pointing at. He was in mid-stride, and as we watched his foot came slowly down. What would have taken less than a second now took a full five seconds.

I could feel the hope for the people inside that machine flood back into me.

Suddenly everyone moved around us.

"Slipped," Patty said, sighing.

"What slipped?" Screamer asked, glancing at us.

"How did you—?" Samantha was looking up at us clearly surprised that we had suddenly appeared in front of her without her new senses alerting her to us.

All the hope I had felt a moment ago drained out like someone had pulled the plug. "Does it slip often?"

She shrugged, looking very upset. "I don't know."

She had the same type of control over her powers that I did over mine. They were there at times, at other times they didn't show, and it often made no sense. Before now I was just happy when any of my weird powers showed up to help me out of a situation. It had never been an issue before to have a power be consistent and controlled completely. And clearly, that had been the same for Patty.

135

Patty looked at me with an apologetic look on her face, as if she had let me down. She and I both knew we couldn't depend on just her power to get those people out of there. Too much chance things would slip at the wrong moment and people would die. So we would use it only as a last resort.

"Can your power back-up my power?" she asked, still holding my hand.

"Never hurts to try," I said.

Keeping a firm grip on Patty's hand, I took a deep breath of the musty-smelling warehouse air, then focused on slipping between two upcoming seconds. That's what it had felt like when Stan had taken me between time, and I tried to bring that feeling back.

"It worked," Patty said, laughing.

I glanced around. Screamer had his mouth open, about to ask a question. Tech had started walking back toward the group, and was now in mid-stride.

I felt immediately proud. I had actually managed to stop time around me. What a cool superpower this one was. Then just as quickly I realized this wasn't really that useful in this situation unless I could do it with split-second timing. None of my superpowers had ever been that on-demand and in my control, and I had no doubt this one was either.

Patty pulled me to a place on the other side of Screamer. "Take us back into normal time."

"Done," I said.

And low and behold Screamer started into his question and stopped since to him we had vanished.

"What the—" Screamer said, turning around to stare at us. "You two can really get on a person's nerves."

"Again," Patty said softly to me, squeezing my hand and giving me balance."

I focused on between seconds and again time stopped around us.

She pulled us around behind Screamer again. "Let it go, then do it again as quickly as you can."

"Practice?" I asked, seeing what she was doing.

"Practice," she said. "We'll work on your power for a few times, then on mine, then see if we can combine them in some fashion to get some safety margins."

Now I saw what she was intending. Her power wasn't safe enough to use alone. And mine wasn't quick enough, but between the two of us, we might get the chances down to acceptable risks for the people coming out of the machine.

I started to feel hope again.

"Here goes," I said. "In and out a few times as quickly as I can make it work."

"Ready," she said, squeezing my hand softly.

I took a deep breath, pushing back the wonderful feeling of having her holding my hand, and focused on what I was going to try. I was going to flick on-and-off a superpower like it was a light switch. I had never tried that before.

I dropped us back into normal time.

"Back here," Patty said to Screamer's back.

I switched us back between seconds.

We moved down the aisle to a position behind where Tech was walking, then I dropped us out again.

Screamer wasn't halfway through his turn when we appeared.

"Sorry, Tech," Patty said. "Just practicing."

Tech jerked and started to whirl around as I took us back between seconds.

This would have been a great party trick if the situation wasn't so serious and so many lives were at stake.

I took us in and out five more times, then stopped with us standing in the middle of a very confused group.

"Stay put for one second," Screamer said.

"That was very weird," Samantha said.

"How did you do that?" Tech asked.

Johnny just sat on the floor and shook his head in amazement.

"Sorry guys," I said, smiling at Patty. "We are just practicing a little to see if we can come up with a way to slow down time enough to get Geneva and Ben and the rest out of there."

"You actually think you can do it?" Johnny asked, climbing to his feet.

"That's what we're trying to figure out," Patty said. "Poker Boy here can stop time. But so far, the best was four seconds apart. I can slow down time, but I can't always hold it."

"So pardon us while we practice a little more," I said. Then I took Patty and me between time, stopping the questions from the others for a moment.

She smiled at me with that wonderful smile of hers, then squeezed my hand. "You're getting pretty good at this."

"But not good enough," I said. "Do you see any way we can combine our two powers to make this safe enough for people coming out? I clearly can't stop and start time three times in one second."

"I think there's a way," Patty said. "But I need to practice my slowing of time, try to figure out if I can sense when my power is about to slip."

I nodded, seeing where she was heading. "If you can tell when your power is about to slip, you can signal me and I can stop time until you can get reset."

"That's what I'm thinking," she said.

"Okay," I said. "Let's practice."

I dropped us back into real time, letting Johnny complete his last step toward the group.

"Who has a measured step?" I asked before anyone could react to Patty and me being in different positions. "We need someone walking a timed pace down the aisle so we can do some tests."

"I'll walk," Screamer said, moving back into a position like he was a racer at a starting line.

"I've got a stop-watch function on my watch," Johnny said. "Will that help?"

"It will," Patty said.

"Five seconds and stop," I said.

A moment later Johnny clicked his watch and said "Go."

Screamer paced out like he was a businessman in a hurry to get to a meeting. About eight paces away from the group Johnny said, "Stop."

Screamer stopped and turned around.

"Good," I said. "Repeat that when I say go. Johnny, time him again."

I glanced at Patty and she nodded that she was ready.

"Go."

Patty slowed time just as Screamer lifted his leg to take his first step and a fraction of a second after Johnny clicked his watch. We moved carefully away from Johnny and Samantha and Tech and off to one side of the aisle.

Slowly Screamer walked back toward us, very slowly. Patty seemed focused inward and I said nothing as Screamer finished his first step.

Then what seemed like an eternity later his second. His third. His fourth. His fifth. He was on his sixth step when Patty squeezed my hand. "It's slipping."

I focused and stopped time right in the middle of Screamer's sixth step.

Patty took a couple of deep breaths.

"You all right?"

"I am," she said. "But it takes focus for me to tell when the power is starting to slip."

"I understand that," I said. "But now comes the part I've been worrying about since we came up with this idea. Can your power work now that time is stopped so I can let go?"

"Let's find out," she said. "Ready?"

"Ready," I said.

"Now," she said.

I let go and let time come back to normal, but time wasn't normal. Screamer was still moving in his slow motion way. I watched as he took his last two steps and then stopped as Johnny's thumb slowly clicked his watch.

"Slipping," Patty said.

"Let it go," I said.

She did and everything came back to normal pace as the group turned to face where we had moved.

"That is so weird," Samantha said again, shaking her head.

"Well," Johnny said.

"I think we can make this work," I said. "We need a little more practice. But one thing we can't test is if we'll be able to pull people out of the chair and maintain our focus on holding time at bay."

Patty nodded. "I don't think I can safely do that."

"I'm afraid I'll get distracted," I said.

"So you're going to need some help," Screamer said. He turned to Johnny. "Think you can sit in that chair without touching that machine?"

Screamer pointed to the ghost slot machine that had everyone and the wooden chair attached to it.

Johnny nodded, took a deep breath and moved to the slot machine.

Screamer took up a position right behind him. "I'm thinking you are touching me, doing your time thing and including me. When someone shows I shove them out of the chair sideways like this."

Fairly gently he pushed Johnny sideways and away from the face of the ghost slots. Johnny managed to stumble but not fall to the concrete.

I nodded and glanced at Patty as both Johnny and Screamer moved a few more paces away from the slot machines. She was nodding also, as if it just might work.

"Tech," I said, turning to the stunned kid standing out of the way to one side next to Samantha. "That machine's lowest payout is three, right?"

Tech nodded.

"How is it triggered?" I asked. I was afraid one of us was going to have to pull the handle and I didn't much like that idea at all.

"Harry can trigger it to pay out from in there," Tech said.

Johnny nodded. "Geneva just asked him and he agreed."

"Can he space the payouts two minutes apart?" Patty asked, slightly ahead of where I was going with my questions. She and I were both thinking we were going to need rest between each use of our powers.

"He can," Tech said.

"He can," Johnny said a moment later.

I looked into Patty's deep brown eyes. I could see worry there, but also a lot of confidence and power. I wouldn't want to try to do this alone, but with her holding my hand, I felt we just might have a chance.

"Okay then," I said, glancing at everyone. "Let's get ready. Johnny, I need you to get some ambulances and police here to help with those coming out. How much longer do we have before these monsters jump again?"

Johnny pulled the sheet of paper we got from The Bookkeeper out of his pocket and stared at it. "Six in the morning."

"Let's hope these things are long dead by then," I said.

I also hoped we didn't have a bunch of dead people at that point as well. It was all a matter of time. And how well Patty and I worked together controlling it.

··◆*18*◆··

THE DRAINING OF A MACHINE

I MADE PATTY and me and Screamer practice just enough to be sure we had the routine down, yet not enough to get us tired. I didn't feel too drained from using my newest-found superpower, but that didn't mean that I wouldn't get tired an hour from now. With two-minute breaks, three people at a time, over one hundred people in the machine, an hour still wouldn't be enough time to have everyone out.

Finally, it seemed as if there was nothing left for us to practice, nothing left for us to do but start the process. I could tell Patty was nervous, and there was no doubt I was scared to death. I was trusting a strange superpower I didn't know I had twenty-four hours ago to save hundreds of people.

I kept thinking I should just call a halt and go get Stan or one of the other gods to help us. Yet another part of me knew that Stan and the gambling gods were watching, and if they didn't think we could do this, they would step in and help. There was a lot at stake for their world as well. That thought gave me a little more confidence.

Not much, but a little.

I did one more quick check of everything we had done to get ready. Johnny and Tech had gone around the warehouse and gotten a number of tarps off of old slot machines. Using those tarps, they had built up a "landing pad" on the concrete floor where people were going to hit when Screamer pushed them out of the chair. I figured it was better than having people sprawl out face-first on concrete.

Johnny had given the police orders to not come into the warehouse. I had asked him to do that because I didn't want to take any chances of a lot of people coming in over the next hour and distracting Patty's and my concentration.

Johnny and Samantha and Tech would help the rescued people to the door of the warehouse. And as Johnny pointed out, Ben and Geneva would soon be with them to help as well.

I hoped he was right. There were so many things that could go wrong.

Ghost slots had taken a lot of people over the years. No one had ever escaped from one before, and we didn't even know if it was going to be possible for that to happen. The people in that machine were just energy in wires. Could they even be reformed into human bodies?

I mentioned that worry to Patty while we had time stopped in one of our practice sessions. She just squeezed my hand in that wonderful way she had of squeezing and said, "There are a lot of things in this world we don't understand and need to just trust. Let's trust this one to work."

"Think Stan and the rest of the gods would show up here and stop us if this was a bad idea?" I asked her.

"I'm betting on it," she had said, smiling that wonderful smile of hers that reached and filled her brown eyes. Then before my mind could drift to my holding a bar of raspberry-smelling soap and her naked in a shower, she had directed me to get focused on practicing again.

I actually managed to stay focused and not think of her. That's how important this was.

"Ambulance and police are here and ready and standing by outside," Johnny said, coming down the aisle from the direction of the entrance.

Tech held up Johnny's watch. "Timer ready."

I nodded. I had had Johnny give him the watch because I had a hunch that when Geneva came out it was going to be painful to Johnny again. Keeping exact timing on this was going to be critical.

Samantha was standing beside the pile of tarps where we hoped people would land after Screamer pushed them out of the chair. She was ready to help, and looking just about as scared and nervous as a person could look. I didn't blame her. Her husband's life was at stake. If this didn't work, he was going to die an ugly death right in front of her.

Screamer moved over and stood behind the old wooden chair that people were going to materialize in. His job actually was going to be the hardest. He needed to push each person out of the way after they had materialized, but before the next person showed up. That was going to be a very physical and rough thing to do, and he was going to have to do it with exact timing.

I moved over to stand beside Screamer facing the colorful slot machines. The image of Saturn dominated everything, demanding that I sit down and just play. The blinking colors, the bright lights were very, very strong draws.

Patty moved up to my left and took my hand. The feel of her wonderful skin against mine allowed me to push the attraction of the machines back into a corner of my mind and away from any bother. Now, instead of looming over me, they were just old machines with a nice design. The feel of Patty's skin against mine was the focus for me.

I reached out with my right hand and grabbed the thin black belt that Screamer was wearing, holding on squarely in the middle of his back. It was the best way to keep in contract with him without restricting his movements in any way.

"Ready?" I asked Patty.

"Ready," she said, squeezing my hand.

"Ready Screamer?"

"As I'll ever be," he said.

"Johnny, tell Geneva we're set to go."

Johnny nodded. Then a moment later he said, "Now."

"Clock started!" Tech said.

I focused on my power as Patty slowed time around us. I needed to be ready to stop time completely if Patty signaled her power was slipping in any fashion.

The next three seconds slid by very, very slowly in Patty's control. Tech and Samantha and Johnny were all outside Patty's influence and moving like a bad slow-motion video.

Slowly Johnny's hands went to his head, as if he had felt a very sharp pain.

Then, in front of Screamer the air started to shimmer.

A vague outline of Geneva started to form, filling in moment by moment in what seemed a very quick time in our sloweddown universe.

Then she was there, fully. Her back was to Screamer, sitting just as she had been when she had gone into the machine.

Screamer, reacting as fast as he could, took her by the shoulders and tipped her out of the chair and onto the tarps. She fell slowly, just as another shimmering started in the chair.

That was close.

Very, very close.

If Screamer had hesitated at all the next person would have started to form where Geneva sat.

I glanced at Patty. She wasn't watching, but instead had her head tipped back and her eyes closed. Her grasp on my hand was firm and solid.

A middle-aged woman shimmered into shape and the instant it was clear that she was all there, Screamer shoved her sideways and out of the chair.

She was barely out of the way and hadn't yet landed on Geneva when the shimmering started again.

Three people in less than one second was almost too fast for even Patty's slowed time. It was very lucky for us that Screamer was reacting as quickly as he was.

Ben, the man Patty and I had watched disappear on the Horseshoe surveillance tapes shimmered into place. Screamer took no chances and shoved him instantly out of the chair and onto the pile of tarps with the two women.

"Slipping," Patty said, squeezing my hand.

I froze time and then said, "Clear."

Patty took a deep breath and looked around at me, then at Screamer and the three people twisted and frozen in place on the pile of tarps. They looked like a twister game gone terribly wrong.

"We got them?" she asked.

"We got them," I said. "But I wanted to have us stay in control of time to make sure no one else was coming."

Screamer nodded. "Make sure the three-payout setting was right. Good thinking."

"Good work on your part," I said to Screamer. "Even with time slowed they appeared faster than I expected them to.

"Me too," Screamer said.

Patty took another couple of deep breaths, then said, "I'm ready."

I wanted us to go another five or so seconds to make sure no one else was coming, so when Patty nodded, tipped her head back and closed her eyes, I slipped us out of between time.

On the mat the three people there were still moving and reacting to being shoved and tangled together, just very, very slowly. It would have made a really funny home video on one of those stupid television programs that made money out of people making fools of themselves.

I had also gotten just a glimpse inside each of their heads as Screamer pushed them aside, but I ignored that.

But the good thing was that all three were awake and alive and moving. And slowly Johnny and Samantha were bending down to help them.

The look on both Johnny and Samantha's faces was something else. Now I can honestly say I have seen pure joy.

Slow motion joy, but still pure.

No one else was materializing into the chair, so I finally squeezed Patty's hand. "We're clear."

She let us slip back into real time.

"Tech, watch that time closely," I said.

Screamer, Patty, and I stayed in positions as Johnny picked up Geneva and hugged her like I had never seen anyone hug before. She was going to be lucky to not have a few cracked ribs.

Samantha seemed to do the same for Ben, holding him and crying.

The other woman, clearly the tourist Geneva had seen being taken from the Mirage, sort of sat there on the tarps watching the scene around her, then glanced up at the Saturn Slot Machines with a look of horror. "Was I in there?"

"You were," Screamer said. "But you're safe now."

The woman scrambled off the tarps and away from the machine.

"Welcome back, Geneva," I said after letting them hug for a few more seconds. "How are you feeling?"

"Headache will pass," she said. "And I know what to do to help."

Samantha let go of her husband and turned to us. "Everyone, this is Ben."

The poor man sort of nodded, then glanced at the machines and stepped back in horror, just as the woman on the tarps had done when she moved away from the machines. I was betting that the people who had been taken were never going to sit down at a slot machine again.

"How long?" Patty asked Tech.

"Seventy seconds," he said.

"Johnny, get this woman out to the ambulances to be checked and then get back here," I said. "Samantha, you want to take Ben out as well?"

"I'm fine," Ben said, "What can I do to help?"

Samantha gave her husband a hug and a huge smile.

"Help Samantha and Johnny and Geneva get the people who are coming out of the machine to the ambulances and police."

"Understood," he said.

Johnny took the frightened tourist by the arm and headed her away from the ghost slots toward the door to the warehouse, introducing himself as he went.

Geneva, Samantha, and Ben stayed.

"Thirty seconds," Tech said.

I turned to face Patty, who was smiling all the way through her eyes. That smile of hers melted me every time, and it started to do it again when Tech said, "Fifteen seconds."

The melt of my very soul froze and I asked her, "You ready for another three?"

Patty took a deep breath and nodded.

"Ten seconds," Tech said."

Patty squeezed my hand, took a deep breath, and tilted her head back and closed her eyes.

"Five seconds," Tech said. Then as we had practiced, he started counting down.

At three seconds Patty slowed time again.

What seemed like a long three seconds later a shimmering started in the chair, right on time.

Three out, almost a hundred left to rescue. It was going to be a long, long grind, and we didn't dare slip even for an instant. If we did, someone would die.

••♦19♦••

NO GOING DOWN WITH THE SLOT

I DON'T REMEMBER ever being so tired.

Over one hour of real time had passed, but with my stopping time on a half dozen different occasions, and Patty's slow time, I wagered Patty and I and Screamer had been at this for almost three or four hours.

So far so good.

The closest call we had was when a very large man showed up in the first in a group of three. Screamer had to almost throw himself with the big guy to the mat to get the man's bulk out of the chair. I somehow managed to hold on to Screamer's belt with one hand and Patty's hand with the other, but for an instant I thought the problem would make Patty lose control.

Somehow I froze time far faster than I ever thought I could, almost like a reaction to the situation. Good to know I could do it that fast, but I hoped to not test it again.

With time frozen all three of us moved around, together, never losing touch of each other, and got the big man's legs out of the way.

Then we got back into position and Patty took over control again and the next two people in that group made it out just fine.

From there the process just went on, two minutes of break followed by slowed time and a feeling of near panic as three people appeared very quickly.

About ten groups ago the man getting off the tarp had told us that Harry was now all alone in the main room. He had been the last one in there helping the old guy stay on his feet.

That worried us all, especially after Geneva had told us how tired and worn out Harry had been. But the next group, and then the next had appeared on time, so it looked like old Harry was hanging on.

Over the last few groups, Patty was having more and more problems, and I had had to stop time twice in both groups to give her a rest. She was getting tired, and I was getting very worried at both of our abilities to keep using our superpower in such a sustained way.

"How many left in there?" I asked Geneva as Tech gave us the sixty second warning.

"If our count is right," Geneva said, "And Harry's count was right, Harry should be the second one out on this next group and that should be it."

"You're kidding?" Patty said. I could hear the relief in her voice.

"We're close," I said, squeezing her hand slightly.

She straightened her back and nodded. "Let's do this."

Tech counted us down just as he had done every time before and Patty slowed time just as she had done so much over the entire rescue operation. Screamer stood ready to push just two more people out of that chair.

But nothing happened.

"Slipping," Patty said.

"Clear," I said as I focused and froze time and let her take a few deep breaths.

"What happened?" Screamer asked. "It's been too long."

I knew that as well. Patty had held that last time slowing a good five seconds longer than what it should have taken to get anyone out of the machine. Harry had been so perfectly on time with everyone before this one.

"We need to keep in slow time and ready," Patty said, "in case he's running just a little late."

I agreed. "Tell me when you are ready."

She tipped her head back and said, "Okay."

I let us come out of between instants of time and Patty had control. This time she held it for twelve real-world seconds, which seemed like an eternity to me as no one appeared in the chair.

"Slipping," she said.

"I got it," I said, again taking us between time.

Near the pile of tarps Ben, Samantha, Tech, and Geneva were looking very worried, their frowns frozen for the moment.

"Not good," Screamer said.

"Harry must have passed out and can't trigger the last group," Patty said.

"Or he died in there," I said.

Patty took a few more deep breaths and said "I'm ready again. "Let's give him ten more seconds before we give up. He'll know not to trigger the payout without exact timing."

I waited until she squeezed my hand to let me know she had it and again took us out of between moments of time and let Patty control.

Ten more seconds and nothing appeared in the chair.

"Slipping," Patty said.

"Let it go," I said.

An instant later we were back functioning in real time.

"I was afraid this might happen," Geneva said. "Harry was so weak."

"Actually," Tech said, "I'll wager the machine needs three to pay out."

"Three minimum?" Johnny asked. "So there's not enough people in there is what you're saying?"

Tech nodded. "Machines don't pay out less than the full amount. Most of these old machines just froze if there wasn't enough to pay a jackpot. An attendant had to be called and the machine refilled."

"Oh, great," Geneva said, "and we're the attendants to a ghost slot machine?"

She had a good point there. We were the ones running this thing, sort of. Actually Harry was the attendant from inside the thing. And now he and some other person were trapped in there.

"I'll go in and get him," Tech said.

I stared at the kid. I hated the idea of him doing that. Hated it.

"You can't," Geneva said. "No communication with anyone out here. I have to go back in."

"Or I do," Johnny said as he strolled down the corridor toward the group. He had been taking the last person of the last group out to the waiting police and ambulances, although so far no one had been hurt beyond being very tired and headachey.

"No, I do," Tech said. "If Harry's too weak to trigger the payout you need someone to do that."

"You can do it through Geneva to me," Johnny said.

"Or through Johnny to me," Geneva said.

I couldn't believe that they were having an argument over who was going to get taken by a ghost slot machine. I had no idea how two people who could hear each other's thoughts could even argue.

That would seem to take all the fun out of fighting. Or maybe make it worse. Either way I didn't really want to find out.

"We can set the timing with back-ups if I go in," Tech said.

All three of them were willing to risk their lives to save the two people in there. It sure showed how really brave the people I was working with were. This was one amazing team that had come together to solve this problem.

Tech, Geneva, and Johnny sort of stared at each other for a moment, then turned to me. They wanted me to decide who would risk their life, maybe lose their life, in trying to rescue the last two people inside that machine. This kind of decision was a lot rougher than trying to decide to lay down pocket kings when an ace hit the board. Or shove all my money into the center of the table on one hand that might get beat and knock me out of the tournament. Those decisions seemed stressful, but nothing like this one.

This one the stakes were human lives, both inside the machine and facing me.

I took a deep breath, reached over and touched Patty's hand and then took the two of us between moments of time.

"Any suggestions on this one?" I asked her, relishing the feel of her skin against mine.

"None," she said, "other than I think it has to be either Geneva or Johnny. We need the contact with the people inside in case something doesn't work out the way we think it's going to."

"Agreed," I said, sort of knowing now who I would pick. Just talking to Patty gave me the strength to act.

I dropped us back into real time and without hesitating said, "Johnny, it would be best if you gave it a try."

"Why?" both Tech and Geneva asked at the same moment.

"Tech, we need the contact in there in case there's something wrong we don't know about, not counting the timing issue. Geneva, you've been through that once already and seem fine. But I don't want to push it twice."

Johnny nodded. "I agree, Poker Boy. "Should I go in here, or wait until the machine jumps in the morning and go in at the casino?"

"Harry's too weak to wait," Geneva said. "I'm afraid he might not last until morning."

"Right here," I said, sounding a lot more sure of myself than I felt. "Let's do this and get this finished."

Johnny bent down and kissed Geneva hard and fast, then turned toward the machine holding up a nickel. "I'll be right back."

As the rest of us moved a few more steps away from the machine, Johnny sat down in the same chair that Screamer had been knocking people out of, dropped the nickel into the machine, and pulled the handle, almost in one motion. It was as if he slowed down and thought about what he was doing he wouldn't be able to do it.

Over the years I had learned that jumping in fast and quick was often the best way to do something unpleasant. Of course, acting like that in a hand of poker had sometimes cost me a tournament. But other times it had won me tournaments. I hoped this time it would be a winner for all of us.

As the first reel on the machine clicked to a stop showing a Saturn, Johnny seemed to jerk, as if getting shocked.

Geneva bent over and grabbed her head.

Ben and Samantha were beside her but not touching her. There was nothing they could do to help her or Johnny at this point.

The second reel clicked to a stop showing a Saturn.

Johnny jerked hard in the chair, not letting go of the machine's handle.

The third wheel clanged to a stop with a sound that seemed to echo throughout the warehouse.

Saturn.

Johnny sort of leaned forward into the machines.

Geneva screamed in pain.

Then Johnny and the ghost slot machines shimmered and disappeared, leaving the warehouse gray and much darker than a moment before.

I stared at the blank place where the slot machines had been, not believing what I was seeing, or *not seeing* as the case might be. The old row of slot machines that filled the wall looked like a row of perfect teeth with a front tooth missing.

"Where did they go?" Tech asked.

Geneva was on her knees staring open-mouthed at the empty place in the row of old, dead slots.

"Geneva," I said, using my most commanding voice, "do you sense Johnny?"

She slowly shook her head.

Then she looked up at me with the most horrific empty look I have ever seen. "He's gone."

··◆20◆··

MATH DOESN'T WORK

I DON'T THINK anything had ever shocked me, at any time in my life, as much as the machines vanishing had done. Yet I knew that's what happened every time a person was taken by a machine.

Why would this time be any different?

Yet I hadn't expected it and I should have.

Now the connection between Johnny and Geneva had been broken, and who knew where the slot machine had jumped to.

Or if it was even coming back.

I needed answers and I needed them fast.

I moved quickly to the pile of tarps, grabbed the top one and swung it around and up over the space where the ghost slots had been. It settled over their form there, just as the tarp that had been over them originally had. We couldn't see anything in that spot, but the part of those evil machines were still right here in the warehouse.

"They're coming back," Patty said.

"That they are," I said as I yanked off the tarp and tossed it back on the pile. "But if my guess is correct, they need a person to jump."

"Not necessarily," Tech said. "They jumped out of here without a person."

I stared at the kid. He was right. They had.

"Where were they headed in the morning?" I asked.

"Johnny's got the paper," Geneva said.

"Circus Circus," Patty said without hesitation, staring at me. "Back wall of the main casino on the far right."

I must have had a very puzzled look on my face because she said, "I know exactly where and when. I memorized the list. Part of my skills."

I had no doubt that was only a minor part of her skills, and I was looking forward to learning a lot more of them, but I didn't let myself go down that road of thought. The ghost slots were loose again and we still had people to save.

"Patty, get on the phone to The Bookkeeper and tell him what happened. Ask him if that changes things on his projections."

She nodded and grabbed her cell phone, stepping away.

"Samantha, Ben, Tech, stay here. Geneva, Screamer, come with me. We've got to get the police to the Circus Circus if they aren't already there."

Geneva, Screamer, and I had taken no more than a dozen steps down the aisle between all the old slot machines when from behind us Samantha said, "Too late."

The three of us spun around like someone had pulled on the same rope. The shimmering of colored lights pushed the gray of the old warehouse away as the ghost slots came back.

And with them the intense desire to sit down and lose myself in their power.

"Johnny," Geneva said softly beside me.

"You two back in touch?"

"We are," she said, nodding and smiling at the same time.

"Thank god."

"Is he all right?" Screamer asked.

"He's fine," Geneva said, beaming like a kid given a long sought-after toy at Christmas. "He just found Harry."

"How is Harry?" Tech asked.

"Weak and very tired, but still alive."

"Fantastic," Screamer said.

"Thanks," Patty said, turning back toward us and snapping her cell phone closed in disgust. The super-powered woman I was in lust with had a lot of emotions, and I sure didn't want the one she was showing right now directed at me.

"The Bookkeeper his old charming self?" Screamer asked.

"He said we're all idiots," she said, clearly disgusted.

"We know that," I said, trying to lighten her mood a little. "But did he say if the machine would stay on the pattern he worked out."

Patty smiled at me and nodded. "It went to Circus Circus and stayed until it got someone, then came back. It's next trip out, unless we feed it someone else, isn't until tomorrow at a few minutes after noon. It will go back to the Horseshoe then, same spot near the stairs."

"And if we feed it again," I asked.

She looked at me with a very funny look on her face. "It will jump to the Horseshoe early is all. But why would we do that?"

I pointed at the machine. "Because right now there are four people in there."

"Oh," Tech said, his voice hushed yet. "The math doesn't work."

"Exactly," I said.

"Oh, no," Samantha said.

Patty just stared at me, her wonderful brown eyes wide. She knew, without a doubt, just as I did, that we were going to have to feed more people to the beast before we had any hopes of saving everyone. Two more people to be exact. One here and one at the Horseshoe.

I glanced around at the shocked team.

Patty and I and Screamer couldn't go in, since we were the rescue team needed to get everyone out. Geneva had to stay out as well since she was the contact with Johnny and Harry inside. That left Tech, Samantha, and Ben. And Ben had already been in the thing once before. I don't think we dared stress him with twice through a ghost slot machine.

"I'll go," Tech said, stepping forward.

"So will I," Samantha said.

"No, I will," Ben said.

"Get Ben to do what I was doing and let me take a crack at it," Screamer said.

In all my years of helping people, I had never seen a braver bunch of people in one room. At that moment I was very, very proud to be working with them.

"Ben," Patty said, "we don't dare send you back inside. We don't know what twice through that thing would do to a person."

"We don't even know the long-term ramifications of once through," I said. "And Screamer, we need your practiced quickness and knowledge of when to get people out of that chair. I don't want to take a chance on someone new at this point."

Screamer nodded. He knew I was right, just as I knew he had to offer to go inside.

Ben started to open his mouth to protest, but Samantha took his hand and squeezed it lightly, some sort of private signal between them that he shouldn't say anything.

I glanced at Patty and she nodded, understanding and agreement in her wonderful brown eyes.

"Geneva, Patty, Tech, Screamer, the four of you go out and convince Johnny's partner out there that he has to take Tech to the Horseshoe. Ben, go with Tech to the Horseshoe and show him exactly where the machines appear. Tech, when you are in position and ready, call Patty."

"I'm going in here?" Samantha asked, her voice firm.

I nodded.

"Now wait," Ben said.

"It's all right," Samantha said, turning to face her husband. "These people rescued you and all those others. They'll get me out as well, along with everyone still inside there. You need to help Tech make sure he's in position so we do this right."

Ben nodded after a moment, then bent down and kissed his wife. Then he said, "I'll be waiting here when you come out."

"Actually," I said, smiling at him. "We plan on having all of them out of there before you can get back here from the Horseshoe. So she'll be waiting for you."

Ben stared at me for a long moment, then nodded.

"Let's go," Patty said. She, Geneva, Tech, Screamer, and Ben headed for the door to the warehouse.

"Looks like all we have to do now is wait," Samantha said.

"The really fun part," I said.

Samantha eased herself down onto the pile of tarps and I sat down beside her. The things were a lot firmer than I had thought they were. More than likely a few of the people we had rescued were going to be very bruised and sore from being tossed on this pile.

"This is a brave thing you are offering to do," I said. "You know we can find another volunteer from the police outside."

"No," Samantha said. "I'm going to do it. I got all these sensory powers from your friend Stan so that I could help. You saved my husband, it's the least I can do in helping the others still trapped in that monster. If this is how I can help, then this is what I'm going to do."

I nodded, gave Samantha a quick hug around the shoulders, then stood, moving over and leaning against an old quarter slot machine across from Samantha. The silence of the big warehouse became heavier with each passing second. The bright lights and colors of the four Saturn Slot machines seemed to call to me, like a bully who just wouldn't give up.

There were four people inside that machine under that giant image of Saturn. Two more of my team were going to willingly go in there to try to save them, under my direction. I just hoped I was making the right decision in letting them.

In all my years as Poker Boy, I had never lost someone who tried to help me. But in all the years, I had never sent anyone into such danger before. Normally I went into the danger myself, making sure the others helping me were safe.

This time, I needed to stay outside of the danger and let friends put themselves purposely at risk so that I could help rescue them and others. Patty and I and Screamer were the superheroes here, yet we really weren't taking any risks.

That didn't feel right.

In fact, it felt just plain wrong. But for the life of me, I couldn't see another way.

And that didn't feel right either.

··◆ *21* ◆··

DEATH AND THE MACHINE

AFTER WHAT SEEMED like the longest time, Patty and Screamer and Geneva came back inside the warehouse, moving toward Samantha and myself at a quick pace.

"All set," Patty said. "Tech and Ben have a police escort to the Horseshoe."

"Good," I said, moving away from the machine I had been leaning against and facing Patty. "How are you feeling?"

She shrugged. "Tired, but fine."

"How about one more quick practice before we send anyone else in there?"

I didn't want to tell her that I had gotten more and more worried about my powers fading. I often had powers for a time outside of a casino, sometimes a few hours, sometimes half a day depending on how long I had been in the casino and charged them up. So I was getting a little worried.

She smiled, her brown eyes taking me in clearly. "I was going to suggest the same thing. You reading my mind now?"

"Not yet," I said. "But there's still hope."

She laughed at my lame joke and then reached out and took my hand.

Again the feel of her skin against mine gave me sensations I never wanted to let go of. Little shivers up my back, along with a warmth inside my gut. It was amazing I had been able to concentrate as much as I had so far.

I pushed the hope of helping her shower with a fresh bar of raspberry soap away and replaced it with the image of my friends dying in front of my eyes because I screwed up. That kind of image will shut down just about any erotic and fancy-filled thoughts, and that's exactly what it did.

"Ready?" I asked, looking into her eyes.

She nodded, tipped her head back, closed her eyes, and slowed time down around us.

"You got it," I said. "Now, let me see if I can still make this work."

She squeezed my hand and said nothing.

I focused on taking the two of us between seconds. For a fraction of a second I couldn't feel anything different, then suddenly it worked, just as it had all evening.

"Got it," I said.

Maybe being around all the old slot machines was like being in a casino. Or maybe Stan had increased my powers like he had with Samantha. Either way, Poker Boy was still in full force and I was damned glad of that.

"Letting go," she said.

She did and opened her eyes. She glanced around at the frozen time and then smiled at me. "I think we're ready."

"I do too," I said, letting us drop back into real time.

"Problems?" Screamer asked.

"None," Patty said.

I regretfully let go of her hand and moved back to the quarter slot I had been leaning against a few minutes before. Samantha looked nervous sitting on the tarps and finally climbed to her feet and started pacing.

Patty watched her for a moment, then moved over to Geneva. "Are Johnny and Harry all right in there?"

"They are," Geneva said. "And Harry completely agrees on the problem with a three person payout. He was afraid that might be a problem, and was hoping we could figure out a way around it. He thinks we're nuts for doing it the way we're doing it, but is thankful we are at the same time."

Since Geneva was connected clearly to Johnny, and he was with Harry, I had a question I had been worrying about. "Did Harry notice anything when the machine took Johnny and jumped? And then when it took the other person at Circus Circus and jumped back?"

"Nothing," Geneva said, relaying Harry's answer through Johnny.

"Good," Patty said. "I had been wondering about that as well? Samantha's and Tech's jumps won't bother anyone then."

"Nope," Geneva said.

Again, the big warehouse went deathly silent as we waited.

There was nothing worse than waiting, and nothing worse than the silence of a bunch of dead, dust-covered machines that once had been active. Only the ghost slot looked alive, its colorful lights filling the space between the rows of dead slots.

I wondered how many other ghost slots were functioning in this building, maybe not active now, but waiting for a little bit of energy, a little bit of attention like Harry had given these Saturn Slots.

Harry's mistake in trying to save himself by getting the machine to pay him back out was the only thing that might end up saving him. His mistake had caused the ghost to keep hunting and take lots of people, even though it had him inside.

And it was the sudden large amount of people going missing that had led us to this place, this moment. Thankfully, most of those people were now safe and back with their loved ones. Only four more to save, but to do that, we had to risk two others to get the total right so that the machine would work.

Patty's phone rang with a Mozart tune that seemed very out of place.

Samantha froze and turned to face Patty.

Patty pulled the phone from her pocket and answered it with a simple, "Yes."

"Good," she said. "You're near the top of the restaurant stairs?"

"Okay," she said, "here it comes."

She clicked the phone off and turned to face me. "Police in position, have the area blocked off completely. Only Ben and Tech are there."

I turned to Samantha. "You ready?"

"One problem," she said.

"What?" I asked, suddenly getting very worried about her.

"Can I borrow a nickel?"

She smiled at our shocked faces, then turned to Screamer who was digging in his pocket.

He handed her a coin. "Safe trip. See you shortly."

Samantha took the coin. Then, with a quick adjustment of her sunglasses, moved over to the machine and sat down, her back to all of us.

"The machines seem very intense, radiating energy in a number of spectrums," she said, fumbling with the coin for a moment before putting it into the coin slot.

"Coin and machine noises are very loud," she said, reporting the experience to us and more than likely keeping herself as calm as possible under the circumstances.

She reached out and pulled down on the metal arm.

"Noises even louder now," she said, turning her head slightly as if listening to the wheels of the slot machine spin. "Almost like voices calling to—"

The first wheel locked down onto Saturn and she jerked with the electrical shock going through her arm.

The second wheel locked down onto Saturn and she jerked again.

The third wheel stopped on Saturn and she slumped forward toward the machine as it took her and vanished.

"I hope I never have to see that again," Screamer said, his voice low and angry.

I felt the same way. I was angry that we had to put Samantha through that.

And scared for her as well.

"You in contact with Johnny?" Patty asked.

Geneva shook her head, the empty and scared look back in her eyes.

"Deep breaths you two," Patty said, turning to face me and Screamer. "There are some brave people risking a lot right now. We are shortly going to have work to do."

Patty smiled at Screamer, then at me. Whatever calming superpower Front Desk girl was using at that moment, sure worked on me. I smiled back at her.

"Ready," Screamer said.

"Ready," I said.

"Now all we need is a ghost slot machine," Patty said, taking my hand.

The three of us stood there, waiting, facing the empty hole in the row of old slot machines, waiting for the ghost slots to come home.

Three superheroes with nothing to do until the enemy showed itself.

Five long seconds later it did exactly that, shimmering back into place, very much alive and radiating light and energy.

The three of us, like a military unit, stepped forward and into position behind the seats of the four slot machines, with my left hand in Patty's right hand and my right hand holding onto Screamer's belt.

"Tell Johnny to tell Harry we're ready," I said to Geneva after getting a slight hand-squeeze from Patty.

"They're ready," Geneva said. "Two minute intervals just like before. I'm timing you. Just say the word."

Patty leaned her head back and squeezed my hand that she was ready.

"Now," I said.

"Triggering payout now," Geneva said.

Patty slowed time as I stood ready to stop time completely for the three of us.

A long few seconds later a shape started to form in the chair in front of Screamer. Just as before, Screamer waited until the very instant Tech was all there, then shoved him out of the chair and onto the tarps as Samantha's form started to take shape.

Samantha was suddenly fully there and again Screamer got her out of the way just in time for a man's shape to start to appear. This was the guy taken at Circus Circus before we could stop it from happening.

Screamer got him out of the chair and onto the tarp with the other two as we waited.

No one else. At least yet.

"We're clear," I said.

Patty let the slowed time drop and the three of us rushed to help Geneva get the people off the tarp.

Tech was still out cold, but breathing well.

Samantha was moaning and holding her head, but she also seemed all right. The man from Circus Circus just looked confused. He was clearly a tourist. He had on a bright red shirt and Bermuda shorts, with white tube socks and black leather shoes. His hair was thinning and his skin was slightly burnt from too much time in the sun on his first day in town.

"Stand over there and don't move," I told the guy, using my best authority voice.

He meekly nodded and backed to a position against the opposite side of the aisle, his eyes wide.

"How much time?" Patty asked.

"Forty-five seconds," Geneva said.

"Here we go," I said.

I turned to Patty. "You ready for one more group?"

"I am," she said.

This time I reached out and took her hand as we moved into position behind the old wooden chairs of the Saturn Slots.

"Ten seconds," Geneva said. "Johnny wants to know if you're ready?"

"We're ready," Patty said, tilting her head back and starting to concentrate.

Geneva counted it down just as Tech had done. "Now."

Patty closed her eyes and took us into slowed-down time.

A second later Johnny's form started to appear in the chair. I could feel Screamer brace his feet and the moment Johnny was fully there, Screamer shoved the big detective hard toward the tarps, barely getting the man out of the way before a young woman started to appear.

This woman had been in the slots almost as long as Harry, and the moment she appeared she was like a wet rag being shoved from the chair.

Then finally, one last form started to take shape.

The Saturn Slots started to hum, the noise even louder in slow time, climbing quickly to a high-pitched sound that made me want to put my hands over my ears. I managed to not do that, keeping a firm hold on Patty's hand and Screamer's belt.

I could feel the pavement shaking under my feet as the ghost slot fought to keep its last source of energy.

Finally, the figure of an older man I assumed was Harry appeared completely in the chair.

Screamer knocked him sideways and onto the tarp with Johnny and the young woman.

He moaned and lay there, breathing.

He was alive.

We had got them all out alive.

In front of us, the ghost slots sat, dark and very silent.

The pull to sit down and play that had been a constant was gone.

"We're clear," I said to Patty, squeezing her hand lightly. "And we're finished."

She opened her eyes and let us slide into normal time.

"It's dead," she said, staring at the machine, her voice sounding almost shocked that we had actually beaten the thing.

"Very, very dead," Screamer said.

I just stared at the ghost slot.

A few moments ago, it had been a dangerous monster. Now it was just four old, worn-out slot machines. Still dangerous, I would bet, but as long as no one played the things, they couldn't harm anyone.

They had no energy, no human to feed them and drive them to take and take and take.

I glanced down the row at all the other old machines sitting along the wall, stacked in rows in the huge warehouse. How many of these slots had taken the life force from someone in the past and now just waited to be fed again?

I suddenly very much wanted to be out of this graveyard and back in the bright lights and activity of a poker room. I very much wanted to be risking tournament chips instead of people's lives.

The Saturn Slots sat there, staring at me with the three reels showing small Saturn jackpots.

I stared back, knowing that this time we had beaten the machine. This time.

But as anyone will tell you in Las Vegas, you can't beat the machines over the long haul.

And I didn't even want to try.

··◆ *22* ◆··

A HAPPY ENDING (WITH FOOD)

AFTER STARING at the dead slot machines for the longest time, Patty put her arms around me and gave me the biggest, most wonderful hug I ever remembered getting.

That hug broke my deep thoughts about slot machines and the nature of life, and took me right to wonderful daydreams about showers and bars of raspberry soap.

Screamer suggested a few moments later, after Patty stopped her hug and let me take a breath, that everyone meet at the diner off Fremont Street.

He said he would go ahead and make sure Madge kept the place open for them.

Everyone agreed, but Johnny and Geneva weren't sure they were going to make it. Johnny had a lot of work ahead of him and Geneva had to report in to her boss Adam, although Geneva said there was no chance she was writing about what actually happened.

Johnny and I and Patty and Geneva had a quick huddle and agreed that no slot machines should be officially mentioned, that the case of all the missing people would just remain an unsolved mystery in the files of the police.

Johnny asked just how he should explain where all the missing people came from. Patty just smiled and said, "Tell them you found them in the warehouse, and if anyone pushes the point, tell them to ask the kidnapped victims where they were, see if anyone believes that."

I had no doubt all this would be the main topic of gossip around town. And Johnny would again be a hero on the force.

Once again, I got him to agree to not mention my name in any fashion. Patty asked for the same thing, and he and Geneva both agreed.

I had never felt such fantastic relief as I left that warehouse and followed Patty quickly to her car, avoiding any talk with any of the police.

One hour later, after a quick shower alone in my own room, I joined Patty and Screamer and Ben and Samantha and Tech at the diner across the street and around the corner from the Horseshoe.

We were the only customers in the place, and the closed sign was in the window. They had pulled a couple of tables together to make a large one right in the center of the place. Madge was waiting on them and was even smiling as she popped her gum and brought everyone drinks and food. I had no idea what Screamer had offered her to keep the diner open late for us, but whatever it was, she liked it.

I slid into a chair beside Patty and she gave me a big smile and a squeeze of my hand.

Her eyes lit up with the smile and the touch of her skin lit me up.

Everyone was laughing and talking and enjoying the moment. After all, it wasn't often you got to celebrate saving the lives of over a hundred people.

Twenty minutes later, to all of our surprise, Johnny and Geneva showed up, walking in hand-in-hand and smiling from ear-to-ear.

"How did you two escape?" Screamer asked before I could as the two pulled out chairs and sat down.

I couldn't imagine how much paperwork Johnny was going to have to do with solving this many kidnappings behind him.

"Dinner break," Johnny said.

Geneva laughed. "We gave them no choice. And it's past the morning edition deadline. Adam wants to take his time on how we come at this one."

"Don't blame him on that," I said.

I could just imagine how bad any decent newspaper would do if they printed a story about ghost slot machines. They'd be the laughing stock of the industry, no matter how much proof they tried to offer. And besides, this was Las Vegas, and the *Sun* was the main newspaper. No smart newspaper would print something that would kill the golden goose. I can see why Adam wanted to be careful and not rush into print with anything.

Suddenly, I felt the now very familiar feeling of time stopping around the table. Madge was on her way across the room, frozen in mid-step. The sound of an old Buddy Holly song was gone.

"Great work, people," Stan said. "You are an amazing bunch, let me tell you. Laverne and all the gang working the casinos sent me to thank you all."

Screamer and I and Patty and Samantha just sat there. I know I was stunned, and by the way Patty's mouth was hanging slightly open, I would have bet she was as well.

Tech, Ben, Johnny, and Geneva just looked confused. They had no idea who this person was who had just stopped time and walked up to the table.

Laverne, Lady Luck herself, had sent her thanks. I had no idea what that meant, but I sure had my hopes.

"I want to thank you, Stan," Samantha said, "for what you gave me."

"You earned it," Stan said. "I hope you and your husband decide to move back here. The security forces of some of these casinos could sure use your special powers, as could those I work with once in a while."

"We were actually talking about that on the way here," Samantha said, smiling at the shocked look Ben was giving Stan.

"Great," Stan said.

Stan then turned and looked directly at me, his gaze cutting through every thought I had.

"Poker Boy, I still owe you for that Christmas thing. Now I owe you for this as well. Don't forget to collect if you need to."

"I won't," I said.

Stan took Patty's hand and kissed the back of it lightly. "A pleasure, as always. I owe you as well, and look forward to your collecting."

Patty had the decency to just blush and say nothing.

Stan then pointed to Screamer. "No rest for the weary."

"What's going on?" Screamer asked, pushing his chair back and standing.

"Police just caught a guy they think buried his wife alive somewhere out in the desert," Stan said. "Sorry to take you from the party, but they need to find out where he buried her and try to get to her to see if she's still alive."

"That's it for me," Screamer said, smiling to the group as he moved to stand beside Stan. "Next time, everyone. And Poker Boy, tell Madge I'll make it up to her later."

He gave me a smile that let me know I didn't want to ask exactly what he was going to make up to Madge.

"Thanks, Screamer," I said.

"Yes, thank you," Samantha said. "For helping bring Ben back to me."

"I'll see you around I'm sure," he said to Samantha. "Maybe we can even work together on a case some time."

"I'd love that," Samantha said.

"Again, congratulations, everyone," Stan said. "And thank you from us all."

With that, the Buddy Holly song started back up, Madge kept coming toward us, and Stan and Screamer were gone.

Patty and I spent most of dinner, between wonderful laughing and bad jokes about old slot machines, explaining who the gambling gods were to Ben, Samantha, Johnny, Geneva, and Tech, and why it was so special to have Lady Luck herself thank us.

It was somewhere in the middle of my mixed-berry pie that Patty reached over and put her hand on my leg under the table.

Oh, at that moment I felt better than if I had won the entire World Series of Poker. So many thoughts, so many emotions were going through me that I just about had a melt-down right there.

Patty leaned over, her hand firmly on my thigh, and whispered softly in my ear. "Don't eat too much dessert."

I wanted to ask her why, but just barely managed to turn and look into her eyes instead.

"I've got a very special dessert for you back at my place," she whispered. "It includes a long hot shower and a bar of raspberry soap."

She pulled back slightly so I could look into those wonderful brown eyes of hers. I could tell instantly that she was very, very serious.

I started to ask her how she knew about the soap and shower of my dreams, then realized that she was a superhero. She was Front

Desk Girl. More than likely, one of her special powers was to sense someone's wants and needs. Over the time we had been together, I had been giving off a lot of clues. Even the most rank of poker players could have read me and my emotions when it concerned her. No doubt her superpowers had me read right from the start.

I pushed the remainder of my pie away with a firm push that sent it into the middle of the table.

She laughed. "I take that as a yes?" she asked.

I put my hand on top of hers and squeezed, then with a smile I turned in my chair to face where Madge was standing and shouted, "Check!"

Later that night, I practiced my new superpower ability to stop time, making the shower and the wonderful-smelling bar of soap last a very, very long time.

The next morning, Patty went back to work, with a promise of a very special late dinner after the tournament was over.

I signed up and played in the three-thousand-dollar-pot-limit hold-em tournament. I got knocked out a little after eleven that evening, after my pair of black sevens caught another seven on the flop to make a set. I got all my chips in and was ahead in the hand until the guy who had called me with a pair of fives caught runner-runner hearts to make a heart flush.

So much for doing favors for Lady Luck.

But that night, staring into Front Desk Girl's wonderful brown eyes, I knew right then and there that I was the luckiest person alive, and sometimes there was more to life than winning a poker tournament.

FIND OUT WHAT HAPPENS WHEN THE SLOTS
OF SATURN RETURN. READ "THEY'RE BACK" IN
FICTION RIVER: FANTASTIC DETECTIVES, ON SALE
NOW. TURN THE PAGE FOR AN EXCERPT.

ᵈ◆ *1* ◆ᵈ

NOT POSSIBLE, BUT FACT

"THE SLOTS OF SATURN are back," Stan, the God of Poker, said to me as he slid into the booth beside Patty.

I laughed and pointed out the window. "Pig just flew by. Pink, a ribbon on its tail. Really flapping hard."

Patty giggled and shook her head.

Stan said nothing, didn't even laugh at my stupid joke.

"Wait, just saw another."

Again he didn't laugh or even shake his head in disgust, which he often did when I got really silly.

Both Patty and I just stared at him, waiting for his punch line. He had just said that the Slots of Saturn were back. That had to be a joke with a really stupid punch line, because those monsters were not a laughing matter.

But no punch line was coming, at least none that I could tell. Trying to get a read on the God of Poker was just about impossible. He had the best poker face on the planet and with his tan slacks, button-down brown cardigan sweater and short brown hair, he could make himself invisible in a crowd without any powers at all.

"Sorry, Poker Boy, Patty," Stan said. "I can't believe it either."

"Serious?" I asked. "No flying pigs with pink ribbons?"

"Serious," he said.

Patty and I had been having a quiet lunch in my invisible office, floating high over the Las Vegas strip. I should have known a wonderful day like today would have a crisis in the middle of it.

Just not this crisis.

Any crisis would be fine except this one.

Patty and I were both dressed in casual jeans and light shirts to spend the day together, since she had a day off from her job at the MGM Grand Hotel front desk. I still had on my black leather coat and fedora-like hat that was my uniform as a superhero. I just didn't feel comfortable going many places without them.

We had plans to tour the Mob Museum that both of us had wanted to see for a year, but hadn't found the time. Then we hoped to have a nice dinner and then go back to her apartment, watch a movie, and see what happened next.

I had been looking forward to that "next" part of the plan all morning.

And lunch in my office had seemed like a great way to start a relaxing and fun day together.

My invisible office floated a thousand feet over the Las Vegas Strip and consisted of four walls of windows and a diner booth smack in the middle of the room. The red vinyl booth had soft seats and could hold eight around the table with room enough for another two to pull up chairs on the end. It was patterned after Madge's imitation

1960s diner my team had met in for years down near Fremont Street in downtown Las Vegas.

An invisible door led from Madge's Diner to this office so that Madge, the waitress (who was also a superhero in the food service part of the gods), could wait on us in here. It was also the entrance for those without teleportation powers.

My office actually served as more of a clubhouse for the members of my team more than anything else. Sitting up here at night on a chair with your feet up on the railing looking out over the city and The Strip was always amazing and relaxing.

After hard days, a lot of the team members did just that.

There was also another invisible door that led to Patty's apartment where we stayed while in town. When we completed our new home we were building in the Oregon Coast Mountains, I would put in a direct door to this office from there as well.

Since Patty didn't teleport, that would allow her to get back to Vegas anytime she wanted from our new home in Oregon.

Patty Ledgerwood, aka Front Desk Girl, was my sidekick and partner and the woman of my heart. We met the first time The Slots of Saturn ghost slots had attacked the city. And we had been a pair ever since.

Now it seemed the ghost slots were back.

Not possible, just not possible.

I just wasn't going to let myself believe it yet.

Madge came through the door from the diner with my cheeseburger and Patty's salad and a big basket of fries. She had already brought us both a large vanilla milkshake to share and had Stan's favorite strawberry shake on her tray as well.

She slid lunches in front of us and gave Stan his shake. Then she slid the fries over to an open spot at the end of the table and turned to leave without saying a word.

The fries only meant one thing. Laverne, Lady Luck herself, was on the way and had ordered ahead.

So the ghost slots really were back, even though that was completely impossible.

A moment later Screamer, the other original member of our team, and Ben, the oldest and yet newest member of our team, appeared and slid into the other side of the booth facing me and Patty.

Screamer had taken part when we rescued over a hundred people from near death in the Slots of Saturn the first time. But wow, that was a long time ago.

Ten years ago, to be exact.

Screamer had the ability, among other things, to get into someone's head and read their thoughts and transfer those thoughts to others. He was a superhero working on the law enforcement side of the gods.

Ben was a god himself, just as Stan was. Ben had been the God of Lamplighters for centuries, but as lamplighters weren't needed as a profession anymore, he had faded. He had spent a lot of time over centuries reading and he remembered every detail. I got him moved over to work with the Gods of Books and Libraries to get him healthy again, and he had become a critical part of our team. He knew history and he knew all the politics and history of the gods. I couldn't believe how much he had helped us so far.

"So what Stan said is true?" I asked, looking at Screamer.

"We got ten people missing so far," Screamer said, nodding, "and my sources with the police think it might be a few more."

"But how?" Patty asked, her voice sounding as stunned as I felt. "We all three stood there outside that warehouse and watched those three slot machines be hauled off to be crushed and destroyed."

I glanced at Stan, who only shrugged. "We don't know, but we've seen security images of the Slots of Saturn appearing and taking someone and vanishing. Just as they did the first time. Exactly, actually. Same spots in the casinos. The locations they appear, that we know about, we now have blocked off."

"So they really are back?" I asked, the fear crushing any idea I had of taking a bite out of my cheeseburger, no matter how good it smelled.

"It seems that way," Stan said. "And we checked and they are not returning to the old Standard Machines warehouse."

"So we don't have any idea where they are stored this time?" I asked. That was how we had managed to deal with them the first time. We found their home.

"No clue at all," Lady Luck said, appearing and pulling a chair up to the table. She didn't grab a fry, but instead just sat there, staring at me.

And when Lady Luck just stares at you, that is not a good sign.

·♦♦ *ABOUT THE AUTHOR* ♦♦·

USA TODAY BESTSELLING AUTHOR Dean Wesley Smith published more than a hundred novels in thirty years and hundreds and hundreds of short stories across many genres.

He wrote a couple dozen *Star Trek* novels, the only two original *Men in Black* novels, Spider-Man and X-Men novels, plus novels set in gaming and television worlds. He wrote novels under dozens of pen names in the worlds of comic books and movies, including novelizations of a dozen films, from *The Final Fantasy* to *Steel* to *Rundown*.

He now writes his own original fiction under just the one name, Dean Wesley Smith. In addition to his upcoming novel releases, his monthly magazine called *Smith's Monthly* premiered October 1, 2013, filled entirely with his original novels and stories.

Dean also worked as an editor and publisher, first at Pulphouse Publishing, then for *VB Tech Journal*, then for Pocket Books. He now plays a role as an executive editor for the original anthology series *Fiction River*.

For more information about his work, go to www.deanwesleysmith.com, www.smithsmonthly.com or www.fictionriver.com.

www.ingramcontent.com/pod-product-compliance
Lightning Source LLC
Chambersburg PA
CBHW032008240626
47153CB00003B/1177